About the Author

Mignon Eberhart's name has become a guarantee of excellence in the mystery and suspense field. Her work has been translated into sixteen different languages, and has been serialized in many magazines and adapted for radio, television and motion pictures.

For many years Mrs. Eberhart traveled extensively, abroad and in the United States, with her husband, an engineer. Now they live in Westport, Connecticut, where she is a member of the Guiding Faculty of the Famous Writers' School. *Witness at Large* is her forty-third book.

Had it not been for the proposed sale of the Essevan Publishing Company, it would have been a typical summer weekend on the Sahib's private island in Long Island Sound. A shrewd, dominating and beloved old man who had run the company for many years, the Sahib had passed on both its management and ownership to his two adopted sons. But Boyd and Tom were bitterly opposed over the sale, and when Mildred, Boyd's shrewish wife, was murdered, Tom was found at the scene with the murder weapon in his hand.

The horrifying events that take place on the fog-shrouded island over the next few days are narrated by Sister, the Sahib's adopted daughter who has always been secretly in love with Tom. To avoid being forced to give evidence against him, she and Tom elope and marry. But on their return there is another murder, and suspicion falls not only on them, but on the guests on the island: Leaf Trace, a historical novelist whose books are no longer in vogue; John Cobwell, the chief accountant of the publishing company; Alice, a beautiful pink-and-blond girl who had planned to marry Tom; and Nadine and George Bronson, who is the prospective buyer of the company.

The shivering climax of this suspense novel is a murderous game of hide and seek which takes place in the marsh and woods of the island. As always in a Mignon Eberhart mystery, the killer unmasked is unsuspected by her readers, and the tangled but convincing plot, skillful characterization and realistic atmosphere of *Witness At Large* explain why she is acknowledged to be one of the great practitioners of the tale of terror.

Recent books by
MIGNON G. EBERHART

WITNESS
AT
LARGE

WITNESS
AT
LARGE

Mignon G.
Eberhart

RANDOM HOUSE · New York

SECOND PRINTING

© *Copyright, 1966, by* Mignon G. Eberhart
All rights reserved under International and Pan-American Copyright
Conventions. Published in New York
by Random House, Inc. Distributed in Toronto, Canada,
by Random House of Canada Limited.
Published simultaneously in Canada by Random House of Canada
Limited

Library of Congress Catalog Card Number: 66-11997

Manufactured in the United States of America by
Vail-Ballou Press, Inc., *Binghamton, New York.*

All persons and events in this book are completely imaginary.

WITNESS
AT
LARGE

..........chapter 1..........

We spent the winters in the house on Seventy-second Street; we spent the summers on the island. When you are very young you feel that your life is safe, that nothing can change it and it will go on forever just as it is. You also feel that you yourself will never change.

At eleven o'clock on a Friday night in June, I would have said that I was a perfectly conventional young woman. I believed that I told the truth; I also believed that I tried to do what was right and to think what was right, which is different and harder. This changed when, later, I went back down the forty steps.

There was a heavy fog that night. I went down the steps cautiously; there were occasional lights about waist-high, but there were treacherous spaces of darkness between the low lights. I had nearly reached the beach when I heard some sort of sound like a hollow thump upon wood. I looked up then and saw Tom. The light which always shone at night from the sea side of the boathouse was dimmed by the fog, but I saw Tom. He was leaning over, crouched down above the water. The fog was thick but I saw a bare white leg flop over the pier and then flop down into the black water again. I knew it was Mildred. I ran down the few steps and across the little beach.

When I reached Tom he was still kneeling, staring down into the black water. Then I saw a hammer in his hand.

He said, "She's dead." I only saw the hammer and I snatched it from his hand.

3

He leaned further over the water. "She's dead—" he said again.

I cried, "We've got to get her out! She can't be dead! She's under the pier. She'll drown." I gripped the hammer and leaned over the water, too, and could see nothing.

I stumbled to my feet. I gave the hammer a hard swing and threw it out into the black sea. I was sure that I heard a distant splash.

Tom was still crouched down, fishing into the water now with both hands. Behind me suddenly the Sahib said, "Good, Sister. Now go to the cottage and keep out of this." He was still fully dressed, so he had not gone to bed.

Tom was getting down into the water. "She's caught under the pier," he said.

I cried, "Be careful, Tom. It's shallow there—rocks—" as if he didn't know it.

The Sahib said, "Go on, Sister. Get out."

Tom's wet dark hair and white face came up above the pier. He was tugging at something which resisted him. "She's caught."

I leaned over to help and couldn't reach Tom or anything. The runabout was tied out at the end of the pier, where the water was deeper, and I could see its black shadow move a little as the waves lapped in against it and the pier. Then Tom appeared again and he had her, holding her by one arm. Her face and hair came up and I could dimly see her head. There was something black and dreadful all along one side of it and her hair was wet and straggled blackly across her face.

The Sahib was breathing hard. "Accident!"

Tom held on to that flaccid arm. "She was murdered," he said. "Go to the cottage, Sister. Call the sheriff. Hurry."

The Sahib put his old hand, which was then as hard as steel, on my wrist. "Don't call the sheriff. Don't call anybody. Go to the cottage. *Wait.*"

I obeyed him although I was not really aware of it, but I must have stumbled out across the beach. Somewhere along the way I picked up my brief case. When the Sahib spoke like that I obeyed him and always had.

I had left the lights on in the cottage. They made a diffused lane which guided me through the little stand of pines. When I got into the cottage everything was just the same. There was the light on the table, the brass shining at the old fireplace, the shabby chintz on the chairs, the red sofa and the old oriental rug. All of it was just the same.

I must have looked at the little clock on the mantel, for I knew that it was just past midnight, which vaguely surprised me. I must have sensed the changes which that short hour or so had brought and I think I knew that nothing would ever be quite the same again.

The telephone stood on the table; I went to it and then crumpled down into the chair. I could have touched the telephone; its shiny surface reflected a little of my white blouse and a smear of red which was my sweater.

Later I went over and over every moment of that June evening. Even then, if somebody had questioned me and forced me to reply, I suppose I could have told what I knew of the night, moment by moment and word for word.

It had been about eleven o'clock and I was in the cottage when I discovered that I had Tom's brief case. Presumably he had mine and they had got confused either on the train when we had come out from town, or in the runabout from Piney Point, where Mildred and Alice had met us.

I was sure that nobody at the big house would be asleep and I wished to take at least a nibble at the new Greenleaf Trace manuscript, so I put on my raincoat and went out into the fog.

It was the kind of fog that creeps up stealthily and suddenly from Long Island Sound and blankets the entire universe. But the cottage was only a little above the tiny beach and the boathouse; there was a stand of pines with a path running through it, leading down to the beach. I left the door of the cottage open so the light would guide me on my way back. When I reached the end of the path I could see the diffused halo of the light at the sea side of the boathouse. I started across the strip of damp sand.

Two other people were out in the fog, in the runabout, idling and smoking. There were two tiny red lights, shining a

5

foot or so apart, from the well of darkness where the old run-about lay rocking slowly in the lap of the waves. A wreath of fog drifted to me, bringing a scent of cigarette smoke.

I wondered then who those two people were. I had a sense of intruding upon them, for nobody called out to me as would be natural, and as I started up the long flights of steps leading to the big house, I felt as if I were under observation. There were scattered low lights along the steps, shaded so the light fell downward. I remember thinking that my raincoat and brief case and blue canvas sneakers must be clear under the first light.

There were a hundred and twenty-three steps from the beach to the porch of the big house; these were broken by landings and a bench or two, but it was still a long climb. By the time the lights from the big house above me grew brighter and I trudged up the steps to the porch, I was gasping for breath.

The Sahib said from the shadows on the porch, "Takes it out of you, doesn't it?"

I said, "I didn't see you. Good evening, sir."

"What do you have there?"

"Tom's brief case. It got mixed with mine, coming out from town. I'm working on the new Greenleaf Trace manuscript." I said this with pride in my new title of editorial assistant to Tom.

"Ah." The Sahib sighed and then tipped his head to one side as if he were listening. I was then aware of the open and lighted windows directly behind him and of voices coming from them. There was a little pause; then the Sahib said, "Oh, yes. The new Leaf Trace manuscript. God sends us these things to try us. Check every historical reference, Sister."

"Oh, yes, I will." I knew Greenleaf Trace's books; they were huge historical novels, very long on romance but danger-ously short on historical accuracy. Once he had been a best seller; he was so no longer, although a certain pretense was kept up and the Sahib was loyal to his authors. The Sahib said, "Leaf has made a great deal of money for us. Treat him kindly. Besides, he's here. Came out this morning. He'll be

6

looking over your shoulder and pointing out the beauty of his dramatic scenes if you're not careful."

"Oh, no!"

"Oh, yes." There was the ghost of a chuckle in his voice. "He shot out the door like a bullet a few minutes ago. Didn't like the family quarrel going on in there." He tipped his head again toward the open windows. Certainly the voices inside the living room were louder and angrier. I recognized Mildred's voice—naturally it would be Mildred's—and then Tom's voice. I couldn't hear the words. The Sahib leaned toward me. "Are you happy, Sister?"

It was so unexpected a question and so difficult to answer that I waited a moment, and the voices in the living room rose. I said, "You've done everything to make me happy. You've been a father to me."

The Sahib pressed my arm affectionately. He said soberly, "I hope that I didn't make mistakes. I know what your grandfather would have wanted you to become. You are my dear daughter, Sister, no matter what happens."

The fact was that the Sahib was not my father, nor Tom's nor Boyd's father, but he was like a father to all three of us. We were a family.

I was sure that he was thinking of Tom's coming marriage to Alice. I was so sure of it that again I found it difficult to speak, and in the pause Mildred's voice from the living room rose in violent crescendo. She shouted, "Your uncle's a senile old man! Boyd's no good in business. *You* can't carry the whole load—you're not that smart. You've got to sell."

I could now see the Sahib clearly, for he moved out from the shadows, leaning forward in his chair so the light from a window fell upon his swarthy, strong face and the white curls below a great expanse of brown baldness. His nose looked very hooked and angry and his black eyes glowed as redly as a cat's. He made some kind of silencing motion with his hand, not that I could have said anything. The Sahib was not young; he had a bad heart; he was retired from business; but nobody called him a senile old man. Except Mildred.

Alice's voice came out, fluting as a bird call: "I'm going

7

back to your place, Mildred dear. This is a family talk."

Mildred burst in, "You're as good as in the family! You promised me to use your influence with Tom!" Her voice was harsh with authority and anger. Mildred, in short, was in the middle of one of her tantrums, and my only impulse was to run down the steps, as Leaf Trace had done, and back to the safety of the cottage. I didn't, for Tom spoke and I couldn't have left just then. "Some day," he said in a measured icy way, "I'm going to kill you, Mildred."

He sounded almost as if he meant it, as I knew he didn't. Mildred knew it, too, for she gave one of her rare snorts of laughter. Alice cried out musically and gently, "I'm going. Goodnight, Tom darling."

"Stay here!" Mildred commanded. "You promised me. You and Tom are getting married. Tell him he's got to sell the company. You like money, Alice. You can't deny that. George Bronson has offered us six million. Tell Tom he's got to sell."

And that, I thought swiftly, might shake Tom's opinion of Alice. But Alice was too smart to say anything, and Tom said, "No!"

"Boyd has the deciding vote, remember," Mildred said, taunting.

That was true. When the Sahib retired he had made it possible for Tom and Boyd, his only two relatives and heirs, to buy the Esseven Publishing Company. But since one of them must have a deciding vote, that had gone to Boyd because he was older and had been the first of us to be given a home by the Sahib. I knew that. Boyd owned fifty-one per cent of the stock.

Tom said, "Boyd won't sell unless you make him do it."

"But it's his decision to make," Mildred said, taunting again. "It's only easier for Boyd if you'll see some sense and agree. Boyd doesn't like to quarrel with you or your silly old fool of an uncle."

The Sahib touched my hand. "You'd better go in before Tom chokes her. She's been like this ever since the prospect of a sale came up."

"I didn't know . . ."

"Oh, yes. She's dug up somebody who wants to buy. He's

8

here now, on the island. He and his wife. Staying at Boyd's house. Name's George Bronson." He gave me a little push. "Go on in before Tom loses his head."

"I only wish he would," I said softly for the Sahib's ear and hoping he would smile and lose that stricken look. I thought it was due more to having heard himself called a senile old man than to the prospect of selling the business.

He grinned just a little, absently, listening toward the open windows. Then the full import of what was going on struck me with utter disbelief and amazement. I felt as if suddenly, like an earthquake, my whole world had given itself a shake. Selling the Esseven Publishing Company was something akin to selling the foundation of publishing itself. It was certainly the foundation and pride of Tom and the Sahib, and perhaps in a lesser degree of Boyd himself. Although Boyd's real feelings about anything were difficult to pin down and understand.

The Sahib pushed at me again, so I opened the screened door to the hall, automatically foiled a moth that desired to enter with me and went as noisily as I could in my rubber-soled loafers over to the bench along the wall where Tom as a rule deposited his brief case. There was the newspaper he'd read on the train as we came out from town for the weekend; there was a pink sweater, Alice's I was sure, and a hammer, but no brief case.

Alice was near the door into the living room and saw me. She said in her gentle, very musical voice, "Oh, here is dear Sister. Have you been here long?"

Her voice was all warmth, but I didn't think she liked me any better than I liked her. Her delicate face, framed with long curly blond hair, was beautiful; she had small regular features, enormous, dark-fringed blue eyes and a softly pink and white coloring. She was so striking that I could see why Tom had fallen in love with her. But then the implication of prolonged eavesdropping on my part reached through to me, and I said stiffly, "I just came in. Tom's brief case and mine got mixed up. I came to get mine."

Tom came to stand in the doorway beside Alice. He said at once, in his usual friendly way, "Mine is in the hell room, Sister. I made some notes on Leaf Trace's new opus."

9

I put Tom's brief case down on the bench. The hell room was beyond the living room, so I had to enter it. Mildred was standing beside the big piano, one hand planted upon it. She wore a red shirt and green shorts which showed her stalwart legs, still untanned and white and very bare-looking. As usual, her hair was black and stiff with lacquer. Her muddy brown eyes seemed a little brighter than usual. She looked at me and said, "Well, if you were listening you know then that you'll soon be out of a job, Little Orphan Annie. Mr. Bronson intends to make a clean sweep. Cut away the deadwood. That goes for that stupid little Leaf Trace and for all the deadwood the firm carries. You, too, Sister."

That stung, for it was true that I was in a position of Little Orphan Annie in my relationship to the Esseven family. Before I could reply, if reply there was, Tom said icily to Mildred, "The business hasn't been sold yet. If I have my way it never will be."

"Poor little Sissy," Mildred said, jeering and watching me, her heavy underlip actually smiling. "A hanger-on for—how long is it? Years and years. And now you can't give her a job, Tom, because you'll have no business. What are you going to do? Just support her without making the excuse of giving her a job?"

Alice gave a kind of gasp and cried softly, "Mildred! You mustn't say that. Why, why it sounds as if you mean that Sister is Tom's—Tom's—" She paused, as if the word she clearly indicated was really too much for her delicacy.

Mildred gave another snort of laughter. "Don't fool yourself, Alice. Why do you think Sister keeps hanging around? My advice to you is to get rid of Sister before you marry Tom."

It was then only a little after eleven o'clock and I was still a well-behaved young lady, so I didn't bite and scratch Mildred —which as a matter of fact would have been an ill-advised undertaking. Mildred was bigger and stronger than I. Tom put his hand hard on my arm, and perhaps that restrained me too. He was very white, his eyes blazing. He said, low, "Leave this to me," and strode toward Mildred.

For a second I was sure that he was going to do something

quite violent, but he checked himself and stood facing her. He had changed from his office gray suit and white shirt and dark tie; he wore brown slacks and a worn gray jacket. He thrust his hands in the pockets of his jacket as if he had to hold hard to his self-control. "You are a very silly woman, Mildred. You're trying to hurt me, through Sister. She's been a member of this family far longer than you. Sister earns her way."

"Hah," Mildred said, snorting again.

Somehow Tom kept his hands still shoved into his pockets. "She's edited two of our best sellers this year," he said, still in that icily controlled way. "She brought in three new authors. Sister has earned her way. She also happens to be kind and sensible and intelligent. That's more than can be said of you, Mildred."

"I'm Boyd's wife," Mildred shouted. "You can't talk to me like that."

"You're a poor wife. You've made Boyd's life miserable. You've—"

Mildred cut in, screaming, "But Boyd is going to sell the company! Boyd has the deciding vote! So just wait till he gets back from London. Bronson is ready with the money. It'll all be settled. And you and your senile old uncle and"—she gave me a muddy brown glance—"and all your hangers-on can make out as best you can. After all, you'll have a great deal of money, so it won't be so bad. Alice agrees with me."

Alice cried sweetly, "Oh, no—" She put her hand, the one wearing the great diamond Tom had given her, on Tom's arm. "Tom, I know nothing of all this. I realize that Sister is—is really like a sister to you. And when we are married— Oh, Tom, I don't think a wife should have anything to do with a man's business."

Mildred's dark eyebrows drew together over the thin bridge of her strong nose. "Oh, don't you, Alice! Oh, don't you! Perhaps your bride, Tom, won't be such a good wife either! You don't really know her very well, now do you?"

Alice's face turned a blotchy crimson. "Mildred—" she began in a choked way, and Tom said, "Alice doesn't like innuendoes any better than I do, Mildred! What exactly do you mean? You've hit at Sister and at me."

11

"No," Alice said, "no. Mildred is angry. But of course" —she looked at Mildred—"if you do mean anything in particular you'd better make it clear."

Mildred did back down a little. "I didn't mean anything. But you did promise to back me up."

Tom said to me, "Go on, Sister. My notes are on the table."

It was, as Tom meant it to be, a chance for me to escape. It was a needed escape; I truly did not want to scream at Mildred as she was screaming at everybody, and in any event there was never an efficient way to stop Mildred once she had got into a tantrum. I slid into the hell room, thankful to Tom. I glanced back and Alice had simply disappeared, which seemed prudent; for once I was in accord with Alice. The whole family, everybody concerned, had a tendency to slide out of the way quick as lizards whenever Mildred fell into one of her tempers. If it is true that a family is ruled by the worst disposition in it, then Mildred was the ruler of the Esseven family and had been since the day she married Boyd.

But not quite the ruler. There was the Sahib and there was Tom for her to reckon with. Yet at the moment she did have the whip hand, and Boyd might sell the business.

I closed the door of the hell room softly in order not to draw Mildred's attention.

There was a light there, and on the long table a yellow pad of paper, the kind Tom used for memoranda. I sat down and flicked away a moth. I had escaped Mildred for the moment, but I could not dismiss her angry yet shrewd taunts, for this time she had really exceeded herself. She was, as Tom said, a silly woman, especially when she was angry. Her jibes at Tom through me were stupid, patently false, and that was all. But the word hanger-on had truth in it. I was in a sense a hanger-on of the Esseven household and had been for many years.

This was for a simple reason which few outsiders would have understood. My grandfather and the Sahib, both publishers, had been the bitterest of rivals and enemies. Their enmity was so well known that it became a legend in their world. Their competition was fierce; throat-cutting and back-stabbing weren't in it. Nothing was too bad for one to attribute to the other. I think, in fact, that both may have been quite open and honorable in their business affairs; still, I wouldn't be too sure of that.

In any event, they fought over contract terms, sales representatives and distribution of books; they stole each other's authors—or if out-and-out piracy didn't work, they bought each other's authors, an extreme measure which sharply pained both my grandfather and the Sahib. They fought over reprint rights, about critics, over printing contracts; in short, they fought. It was rumored that once they came to blows at the Dutch Treat Club, but I never knew anyone who had actually seen this. But they fought so long and with such hearty zest that when my grandfather died the Sahib was inconsolable.

He found out then that in his later years my grandfather had not prospered. He had had a long illness, he owed the banks, he owed everybody—and the Sahib behaved in his own quite natural way. He was not called the Sahib for nothing. He had never visited India in his life; the origin for the name was lost in the mist of years, but it fit him in a peculiar way and everybody in his world spoke of him as the Sahib, only that. He was generous, he always had a certain *brio* and he was also the kindest person I had ever known. He swept everything before him; disposed of some rather distant relatives of my father's who perhaps didn't really know what to do with me, a strange child, anyway; had himself appointed my guardian and took me to live in the Esseven household with himself and Tom and Boyd, and a housekeeper and for a while a governess to supervise me. He tried to help straighten out my grandfather's affairs. When it was all over a modest trust fund for me was salvaged; this put me through school with, I always suspected, a generous assist from the Sahib.

The impulse which induced him to take on my care was wholly kind and generous; he had taken on the care of Boyd, many years before, and later Tom. Each of them happened to be left without a home and parents. The Sahib's motives were impeccable, but also the two boys were in fact his next of kin. Tom was his nephew and Boyd was the son of a cousin, but both bore the Esseven name. The Sahib naturally wished to

13

pass along the business he had begun to somebody of his own blood and name. He had legally adopted Boyd and Tom, and both spoke of him as Uncle or the Sahib.

There was no secret about the three children the Sahib had taken into his home and into his heart, but people thought and spoke of us as a family—even people very close to us who knew, if they ever remembered, the facts. Once, in an unusual moment of sentiment, the Sahib had told me that he'd never had time for marriage but that his own children could never have been dearer to him. As for me, I loved him dearly from the first moment when he put me on his lap, gave my hair a gentle tweak and said that he had two boys but he had always wanted a girl. He took me then to a drugstore for an ice cream soda, which must have been both a terrific concession and a terrific shock to the Sahib, who had his small snobberies about restaurants, wines and tailors.

He called me Sister so that, I realized later, I would feel wanted. It became my name.

I had always known what I wanted to do when I finished school; I had cut my teeth on the publishing business and I wanted to work for Tom. So I was given a job in the Esseven Publishing Company. It wasn't much of a job at first, of course. But I did advance, and while my closeness to the Essevens didn't check that advancement, I really did work for it and none of my fellow employees seemed to grudge it when that winter I had been promoted to the post of editorial assistant to Tom. I was happy, until Alice entered Tom's life and thus mine.

Mildred had brought Alice to the Esseven house during the early spring. Tom saw Alice and Alice saw Tom.

Another moth came flittering around the lamp and I brushed it absently away. The room around me was, like the island, familiar and loved. It was called the hell room for several reasons. First it was the room where the Sahib had administered discipline to Tom and Boyd and me when we were young. A summons to the hell room meant trouble for us. It was, too, actually in the shape of an ell, which someone at some time had built out from the living room. And it had been for years the

14

Sahib's study and thus the scene of what the Sahib called hellishly hard labor over the years. The Sahib still used it for a study during weekdays; on weekends it was tacitly turned over to Tom.

The hell room was always in a certain state of disorder. Books in bright new dust jackets were stacked here and there amid piles of papers and odds and ends of publicity notes and advertising layouts; there were clippings and the scattered notes the Sahib made whenever an idea struck him. He had retired, but he would never lose his passionate interest in the business he had made. It was vital to him; it was his lifeblood.

And Mildred proposed to sell that business. It didn't seem possible that her influence over Boyd, strong as it was—mainly because she was a far stronger character than Boyd and she never gave up once she set her mind upon anything—could induce Boyd to agree to the sale. Yet I knew that it was possible.

The Sahib and Tom would try to block such a sale. But when all was said and done Boyd had the voting power to make the decision. And Mildred had already made the decision.

But now, scarcely an hour later, Mildred was dead, her head with its wet black hair stove in like a boat, and I was sitting at the telephone, unable to decide whether or not to call the sheriff and tell him that Mildred had been murdered.

..........chapter 2..................................

Perhaps it was then that I began to retrace the past hour more minutely. In the hell room, after a time, I had got my roiled-up emotions under control, and reminded myself that I did earn my way and that I'd better copy Tom's notes.

It took some time, for it was hard to concentrate. I did not hear any more sounds from the living room, or indeed from the house. When I had finished copying, pausing now and then to relate Tom's points to what I already knew of Leaf Trace's manuscript, I stuffed my own notes in the pocket of my raincoat and took up my own brief case, which stood on the table.

I went out through the living room; now no one was there. I went through the hall and noted idly that Alice's pink sweater was no longer on the bench. I went out onto the porch. I had a vague impression that somebody, the Sahib or perhaps Leaf Trace, was sitting in the deep shadows, beyond the lighted lane coming from the living-room windows. Perhaps there was the slightest creak of one of the old wicker chairs or some shuffle of feet, but nobody spoke to me. I went on down the first flight of steps. The fog seemed to me even heavier. There were misty halos around the low lights along the steps, and there were gulfs of blackness between them, so I felt my way down carefully, taking my time, holding the wet railing and pausing at the landings. I stopped on the last few steps mainly to shift my brief case from one hand to the other.

16

I couldn't see anything but mist for a moment, a few streaky and diffused lights from the house above and the low lights along the steps. But then I heard something that sounded as if someone had kicked against wood. And I had seen Tom, his dark head bent over, kneeling and struggling with something in the water. I saw the thick white leg clad in dark shorts flop suddenly up out of the black water, touch the pier and slide back into the water, and knew that it was Mildred. But Boyd couldn't have murdered her!

I don't know how long that fact had been hovering around me. Boyd had reason to murder Mildred, if there is ever a reason to murder. He must have grown to hate her. But Boyd had gone to London the previous week, so he couldn't have taken a hammer in his hand and stove in her skull.

Tom had had a hammer in his hand, but Tom hadn't murdered her. So I knew then why I had snatched the hammer out of Tom's hand and hurled it out into the black night and the black sea where it could never be found. Yet I hadn't consciously thought of such a thing as evidence, say, fingerprints. I hadn't consciously thought: It is a murder weapon but it could be evidence against Tom. Boyd couldn't have killed Mildred and Tom hadn't killed her. So who had killed her?

Sometimes as a child when I'd been swimming under water and holding my breath a little too long so that I was dizzy and confused and didn't know exactly where I was, I would struggle wildly to the surface and get my breath and look around me. I had much the same sensation then, for I began to look around me and I didn't like what I saw. There were too few people on the island. Indeed, there were only myself, Tom and the Sahib; Mildred and Alice; Greenleaf Trace and Mildred's two guests, whom I had never seen, the man named Bronson, who wished to buy the business, and his wife.

There was not, even, new and strange domestic help. Mrs. Mapping, who with her daughter Henrietta saw to the Sahib's comfort and had done so ever since I could remember, came every morning except Sunday, dashingly in an outboard, cleaned and cooked furiously all day and departed, as dashingly, at night.

Tom hadn't killed Mildred. I couldn't conceive of the Sahib

17

killing her. Besides, the blow which had stove in her head would require a certain strength which I doubted the Sahib possessed. Alice was Mildred's friend; Mildred, indeed, had invited Alice to spend the summer as Mildred's guest so Alice could be near Tom. It was true that they had come very close to a mysterious kind of quarrel that night, in the living room of the big house, but they had swiftly made up again. Alice could have had no reason for killing Mildred even—again—if she'd had the strength and will to do so.

There was no way to make the dreadful estimation of just how much strength it took to smash a woman's head with a hammer. There was no way to surmise anything at all about the two guests, the strangers, or why one of them might set out to kill Mildred.

It was possible that there was some guest in the big house whose presence I was not aware of. Usually John Cobwell came. He had worked for the Sahib since the start of Esseven Publishing Company. He was probably the Sahib's closest friend. But if he was there that night he had come out by an earlier train than the one Tom and I had taken. Of course, there was Leaf Trace, who had shot out of the house like a bullet, the Sahib said, when Mildred's quarrel with Tom began. By no stretch of the imagination could I envision Leaf facing Mildred at any time, let alone when she was in a rage. Perhaps he was not afraid of his own shadow, but he was afraid of everything else.

The list was too short. The island was too small and there were only the three houses on it: the big house, Boyd's new house, and the cottage.

I don't know when the Sahib bought the island. He and Boyd and Tom were already established there when I came into the family. It was called Scatawan Island, which the Sahib said was an old Indian name, but nobody knew quite whether that was the truth or one of the Sahib's improvisations, tossed out with such authority that everybody believed him, or pretended to believe.

The big house stood on the outcropping of rock at the west end of the island. Boyd's new house stood a little below it, on the south shore. The cottage stood beyond the pines, quite close to the boathouse and pier and the small beach which was man-made by sand brought over from the mainland. When the Esseven Publishing Company had a good year financially, this sand was sometimes renewed. The east end of the island was low and marshy.

In recent years the cottage was tacitly considered my own special domain. This was, in fact, Mildred's doing, for after she and Boyd were married and had built their new and glittering house, and after Mrs. Mapping and her daughter had decided that they wished to commute between Piney Point and the island rather than to live on Scatawan, Mildred had raised objections to my presence in the big house. It didn't seem proper, she had said, a young girl living with two men, the Sahib and Tom.

The Sahib had got an evil twinkle in his eye and said that Mildred flattered him. Tom had stared incredulously and then laughed outright. The Sahib said that certainly in the cottage I would be freer to live my own life, and had said it with a wicked implication which infuriated Mildred. Still, I did take up residence in the cottage to which I had no right. But then I had no real claim upon the Sahib. As soon as I had got a job and was in a sense on my own feet I had found a small apartment in town, but I always knew that the cottage on the island was reserved for me.

The island was too small and the list of people on the island was too small and someone had taken a hammer and smashed Mildred's skull and—somewhere recently, sometime that night, I had seen a hammer.

Then I remembered it, on the bench in the hall of the big house, along with Tom's newspaper and Alice's pink sweater. It was the same kind of hammer I had tossed out into the sound without stopping to wonder why I did it.

It was heavy. It was what is called a claw hammer, with one end divided into two strong prongs and the other end solid, but either end suitable for—well, for fracturing anybody's skull.

I tried to remember whether or not the hammer had still been on the bench when I left the big house and started down the fog-shrouded flights of steps to the beach. But I wasn't sure. It could have been the hammer which lay, I hoped with all my heart, lost forever, far out to sea. But if it was the same hammer, then who had taken it from the big house to the pier? Who had met Mildred at the pier? She couldn't have walked, she couldn't even have screamed, after being struck such a hideous blow.

The cottage seemed very still, yet alive, too, with all my whirling thoughts.

My hand went out at last to the telephone, for Tom was right and the Sahib was wrong.

Then my hand jerked back as if it had touched a hot coal. The sheriff would question me. I had seen Tom bending over Mildred, and he'd had a hammer in his hand. A murder weapon.

If I told the sheriff, if I told anybody, what I had seen, if eventually I was forced to tell a jury what I had seen, the jury would be almost forced to convict Tom of murder.

There was a soft knock at the door, and my heart thudded in my throat. For a second I was perfectly sure that it was the sheriff and that he had mysteriously got wind of Mildred's murder and was coming to question me before I could get my story ready for him.

I couldn't move. But then the knock was repeated and I knew it was not the sheriff who had knocked; only Leaf Trace would knock so timidly.

I didn't know what to do. The Sahib had said, "Wait," and he meant wait, don't tell anybody about this yet, don't do anything.

Leaf gave the door a tentative little push and said, wistfully, "Sister?"

So I had to say, "Come in." Besides, I had not drawn the curtains over the window and he must have seen me.

Leaf came in, rubbing his long fingers over his wet mole-brown hair. He was a little man, with a little chin but an enormous nose and forehead; his eyes were enormous too, pale gray and rather vacant. He always dressed rather peculiarly. I never felt that this oddity was a pose; he simply had unusual taste. That night he was buttoned up to his little chin in a black leather coat which glimmered with wetness from the

20

fog. He said, "I saw you, so I knocked. I wondered if you're working on my new novel."

The Sahib and Tom would be coming soon. I must get rid of him. "No, I'm not, Leaf. I haven't read a word of it yet."

"Oh, but I wanted to be sure that you understand the significance of the scene at the guillotine."

"I am sorry, Leaf." I thought with dismay even then: It's going to be French Revolution this time. "I really haven't had a chance at it."

He was immediately apologetic. "I wouldn't hurry you. Dear me, it's a horrid night, isn't it. I've been out and about the island, sitting on a rock on the south shore. Mildred—" He paused, coughed and looked worried. "I hope I haven't caught cold!"

"You'd better go back to the big house and take some whiskey. You do look chilled. Heavens, Leaf! Pneumonia!"

The word was enough. He gave me a wild look from those wide and vacant eyes and scurried out, barely pausing to say politely, "Goodnight."

He had disappeared before it struck me that I had not been so bright in getting rid of him. He'd have to cross the beach, and even Leaf might take note of the Sahib and Tom and whatever they were doing. He might come over to the pier and ask questions.

Then I wondered exactly what the Sahib and Tom were doing. It seemed to me that it had been a long time since I had stumbled into the cottage and gone to the telephone and then had not called the sheriff. I looked at the clock and it was still only a little after twelve, which seemed so unlikely that I went to the clock and listened. It was ticking away sedately as it had for probably a hundred years.

There was another knock at the door, and before I could move, John Cobwell opened it and thrust in his pink, wrinkled face and gray mustache. "Was that Leaf I saw running like a rabbit?"

"Yes. He got the idea that he was threatened with pneumonia. Come in, John."

He came in, shed a raincoat, then laughed shortly. "Poor old Leaf. His heroes are so brave. I saw your light. You must be working late. Mind if I get myself dried out? It's very chilly and damp."

He dropped the raincoat over a chair and sighed. "I've been all over this island. Mildred came to the big house after dinner and I could see she was loaded for bear, so I got out. I don't know whether it's safe to go back there now or not."

It was safe; it was horribly, unbelievably safe from Mildred forever.

John looked washed out from the fog; he always looked washed out. His faded blue eyes gave me a mildly inquiring glance and then sharpened. "What's wrong?"

The Sahib would tell John. Still I hesitated. I said, "I didn't know you were here." John was slightly deaf. He cocked an ear at me, and I repeated it. "I didn't know you were here."

"I got the early train. You'd better tell me what's the matter. You look scared out of your wits. Come on, sit down there."

I sat down, but didn't know how to say it. He waited a moment, then got his pipe out of a sagging gray tweed pocket and began to fuss with filling it from a little zipper pouch, waiting for me to find words.

In a sense John and I were in the same category in relation to the Esseven family; that is, we were close to the family but were not Essevens. John was and had been for years the head of the Esseven Company accounting department. In literal practice, however, now he was called upon concerning legal problems more than for anything else. The company retained a firm of lawyers, of course, but first John was privately consulted about everything; he called himself a curbstone lawyer, his mild blue eyes smiling a little. He eyed me then, fished out a match pack and said, "Well, made up your mind?"

I thought of saying, "You'll never have to run from Mildred's tantrums again." I said, "Mildred—there was an accident—"

He lifted his eyebrows. "Good," he said lightly but then looked hard at me. "What do you mean?"

"The Sahib—Tom had better tell you—"

His wrinkled face seemed to tighten. "It must be serious. Where are they?"

"Down at the boathouse."

He put up one hand, listened, went to the door and opened it. The Sahib came in, his green suede jacket and green scarf looking dramatic and out of place below the sudden deep lines in his face. His dark eyes flashed to John. "We're in trouble."

Tom came in after him, drenched from his recent immersion. He went past his uncle and took up the telephone, and the Sahib said, "No! Listen to me first."

John slid across to the table as quickly as a lean gray cat and put his hand on Tom's. Tom jerked the telephone away, and John said, "Better listen to the Sahib, Tom. Whatever it is, a few more minutes can't change anything."

"It's murder," Tom said. "Mildred was murdered."

John's baggy tweeds seemed to hang there, in the air, without anybody in them. His bent gray head was perfectly still too. The Sahib said, "Make us some coffee, Sister."

I did. Hurriedly, glad to escape, I stumbled into the little kitchen off the living room, measured coffee, put on the coffee pot and set up a tray with cups and saucers and sugar. I could hear the men's voices from the next room, telling John. "I found her there," Tom said. "I walked down the steps and was crossing the beach when I heard something, it sounded like, I don't know, just thumps on the pier. A hollow sound as if somebody was—well, kicking it." He sounded rather sick, but went on. "I ran over to the pier. I could see Mildred in the water, half under the pier, close to the beach. I think she must have been dying or dead then. I got hold of her and pulled her up almost on the pier, but she slid back. There was a hammer on the pier. I stumbled over it and picked it up. Then Sister came and the Sahib came and I got Mildred up out of the water. She'd floated completely under the pier. She was dead. She had a great wound on her head. She—"

John cut in. "Where's the hammer?"

"Somebody—why"—Tom sounded surprised—"why, I guess it was Sister, threw it away."

The Sahib said dryly, "It was Sister. Smarter than you, my boy."

"Where'd she throw it?" John asked. "Out into the sound?" Somebody must have nodded. "I hope she got a good hefty swing to it."

23

"Oh, that's all right," the Sahib said. "It's deep out there. John, we can't report this to the doctor or the sheriff or anybody. We've got to say it was an accident. We've got to wait till morning and find Mildred then. And Tom and Sister have got to get out of town."

"You mean off the island," John said slowly. "How much did Sister see?"

I went to the kitchen door. "I saw Tom—he was . . . just as he said. He was trying to pull Mildred out of the water. I don't think he really knew that he had the hammer in his hand. It's just as he told you. He didn't kill her."

The Sahib's dark eyes were hollowed with shadows. "But your testimony would be the end of Tom, Sister."

"My—but I won't tell anybody."

"You'll lie?"

"Yes, of course." The coffee was bubbling. I went back to the stove and said over my shoulder, "Of course I'll lie."

They waited, all of them, Tom standing at the table, his hand still on the telephone, staring down at the old red and blue rug. I carried the tray to the table beside him, and turned to John and the Sahib. "They can't make me say Tom killed her, because he didn't."

Tom lifted his head and gave me a long and very serious look. The Sahib made a tent of his knotty fingers and regarded it. John said, "Well, then, who killed her?"

"Tom didn't," I said. "I told you."

The Sahib seemed to address his fingers. "You told us what you saw, Sister. Do you honestly believe that a jury, if it came to that, would acquit Tom after hearing what you saw?"

"But I'll not tell that! Not to anybody. I'll lie, I'll say . . ."

The Sahib shook his bald head with its rim of shining white curls. "You'd try to lie. You'd try very hard. I trust you for that. I don't trust you to do a good and convincing job of lying."

John sat down in the rocking chair and hunched forward. "Now do I understand you?" he asked the Sahib. "You want to get Tom and Sister out of the way—off the island entirely until this blows over."

Tom said harshly, "It can't blow over."

"Wait a minute, Tom," John said. "Now then, I gather that

24

the idea is for somebody—you or me, Sahib—to find Mildred in the morning and call it an accident. Right?"

The Sahib merely nodded, but his dark eyes met John's gaze with the effect of communication. John nodded slowly. "Is the wound in her head consistent with an accident?"

"Oh, for God's sake," Tom began, and the Sahib snapped, "Wait a minute, wait a minute!" He turned to John. "Yes! Who's to say that she didn't slip off the pier in the dark and hit her head on those rocks under the pier?"

John clutched his knees and rocked back a little. "Well, it could have happened. Mildred was a good swimmer, though."

"The water's shallow there. A blow on the head . . ."

"What about water in her lungs?"

I felt a little dizzy and sick. I poured coffee and took a cup of it to the Sahib. "If she drowned," John said flatly, "there might be water in her lungs. Or, I don't know, throat choked up. If she was killed before she went into the water, I think there wouldn't be anything much. I'm not sure. But it might make a difference."

"Yes," the Sahib said thoughtfully. "Yes, I can see that. Well—" I could tell that he had made up his mind. "We'll have to chance it. If they have an inquest . . ."

"They may," John said. "Depends on the medical examiner. Accident—nobody supposed to have seen anything of it."

"All right, then. All right," the Sahib said testily. "She fell and struck her head, but it didn't kill her instantly; she came up out of the water, not dead but unconscious; she'd have breathed certainly. But then she slid into the water again. It'll hold together. Nobody can pinpoint precisely the very instant when a person dies from a smash on the head like that."

Tom picked up the telephone again, and the Sahib said sharply, "I'll not have it! Listen to me, Tom. I'm an old man. I'm a sick old man. Everybody knows that Mildred made Boyd's life miserable."

"There's no question of Boyd's having killed her," Tom cut in. "Boyd's in London."

There was a little silence. I poured coffee for John and for Tom. John took it absently. Tom said, "Thanks."

It seemed to me again that John and the Sahib were communicating without words. But then the Sahib said, "Everybody knows, or could easily discover, the fact that Mildred wanted to sell the business. And of course in the end, no matter how hard Boyd fought it, probably he'd have given in. Everybody knows, or would know if they knew this was murder, that you, Tom, were determined to prevent the sale. Only tonight I heard you say that some day you'd kill her. Of course you didn't mean it."

"I'm not sure," Tom said grittily. "I'm not sure I didn't mean it."

"John," the Sahib said, "make him see."

John slid one foot out of a shabby loafer and eyed it thoughtfully for a moment, then shook his head. "It'll be bad, Tom."

Tom whirled on him as if he might shake him out of his baggy tweed clothes. "You can't believe that anybody is going to accuse me of murder!"

John was unperturbed. "Wouldn't surprise me, Tom. Maybe you'd better listen to the Sahib."

"But what you want to do is against the law!" Tom cried. "You've got to report a murder or a violent death."

John said, "Yes. Yes, you do. I'm not at all sure that you can get by with this plan of yours, Sahib."

The Sahib said, "We've got to. You can't report this, Tom. You can't do this to me."

John sipped his coffee, made a little face as if it were too hot and said, "At best they'll call it an accident. At the worst they'll say it's murder and ferret out the fact that Sister found you bending over Mildred with a hammer in your hand. That'll be it, Tom."

"I can't stand it," the Sahib said feebly—so feebly that I looked at him with sudden suspicion. I loved the Sahib dearly, but I knew too that he was not above taking every possible advantage of his illness and that he was as wily as an ancient and rather evil monkey. Tom's dark head jerked up as if he shared my suspicion. And then it came, smooth as silk. "So we'll remove you, Tom, and we'll remove Sister as a possible material witness against you. A wife can refuse to testify against her husband."

.........chapter 3...............................

Tom said in a stunned way, "A *what?*"

John's mustache lifted a little; his faint grin was admiring. The Sahib contrived to look even feebler; I'm not sure he didn't make the hand holding his coffee tremble a little. "It's the only safe way. Take the runabout to Piney Point, get the two o'clock train—elope. Wire me the news of your marriage and where you are staying. I'll wire or phone to you and tell you that there's been an accident and that you must come home. That'll be all there is to it."

"You're out of your head! I think you're . . ."

"Don't call me senile!" the Sahib lashed at Tom, swift as a rattlesnake. "That's what Mildred called me!" He looked at John. "What do you think of it?"

"Well, of course it's going straight against the law."

"Pooh," the Sahib said clearly.

John shook his head reprovingly.

The Sahib's white eyebrows went down. "Don't make obstacles! You've got me out of other problems!"

"Not murder." John sipped more coffee and rocked cautiously, holding the cup so the coffee would not spill. Finally he said, "It might be an answer, Tom. If they call it an accident, then no harm's done. But chances are that somebody's going to wonder about this accident and ask questions. If they do, we'll have the one witness who could really hurt you, Tom, sewed up tight."

I found my voice. "But I wouldn't hurt Tom! I wouldn't testify against him—"

The Sahib's angry look changed to one of loving tenderness and instantly put me on my guard again. "My dear child," he said, "of course you wouldn't. That's what I said. You'd do your best to lie, I can trust you for that. Tom can trust you for that. But I cannot trust you to lie successfully. One wrong word—my God, one wrong look, one quaver in your voice, one instant's hesitation on your part and they'd have you—and they'd have Tom."

"But I can do it," I said stubbornly. All the same I was uncertain. Thinking in advance about the lies you determine to tell is a quite different thing from telling those lies, under oath and on the witness stand and when it is so terribly important to tell the right lie at the right time.

The Sahib said, still with that loving tenderness in his voice which he overplayed only a little, for he really did love me, "Come here, my dear. Come here."

Tom said, "He's going to talk you around, Sister."

But I went to the Sahib because he held out his old hand and I thought of all the kindness and generosity I'd had from that hand. He pulled me down so I was half kneeling beside him and put his hand under my chin. "My dear," he said, with perfect, deadly diplomacy, "I realize what I'm asking of you. Marriage to Tom, a formal kind of marriage to protect my boy. I'm a selfish old man."

"You're an old fraud," Tom said behind me. Boyd would never have said that, but Tom and the Sahib said what they chose to say.

The Sahib shook his head gently, looking down at me. "You're not to undertake this course to save Tom in order to pay me any debt you may fancy you owe me. It's been enough reward to me just to have you in my house, like my own child, to watch you grow up, to take pride in everything you do. No, you mustn't for an instant think of any debt to me. You've repaid anything in the world you may think that I've done for you a thousand times." He leaned over and brushed my cheek with his lips, which were indeed rather unsteady.

It was good acting, part of it. Part of it was not acting. All of it was perfectly devastating. He had used a big gun, and he knew it.

John knew it too; he tipped back in the rocking chair and finished his coffee. Tom said, "Oh, for God's sake, Sister, get up. Don't let him take you in like that. He's trying to get his own way. He's working on your sympathy."

The Sahib said sharply, "I'm doing nothing of the kind. I'm trying to save you, Tom. And you haven't got the sense to know it."

Tom sighed. "I've got the sense all right. I just don't think it will work. For one thing, they're going to know it's murder."

John said, quietly, "But that's the reason your uncle wants you to leave and to have a good reason for it, an elopement. That's the reason—"

Tom cried, "It is murder! Don't you *want* them to find out who did it?"

There was a sudden silence. I got to my feet. Now I was sure that the Sahib and John were consulting without saying words.

Tom looked from one to the other. "What is it? What do you know?"

"Boyd is not in London," the Sahib said flatly.

Tom's face turned white. "But he *is!* He left Wednesday, he's got to be in London."

John said, "No, he isn't, Tom. Henry Walsh went instead. I signed the voucher for his travel money."

"But you—but Boyd—" Tom wiped one hand across his face. "But then—why?"

The Sahib's dark, smart old eyes were very alert. "Boyd talked to me last weekend. He was tired. Nerves shot. I told him to send Henry Walsh to London. Henry is as likely to get business done there as Boyd, far more likely than Boyd in his present state of mind. So . . . That's all."

Tom stared. "Where is Boyd?"

The Sahib sighed. "He's out in his cabin cruiser. I really don't know where."

Tom looked stunned. "His cabin cruiser's getting an overhaul. It's at Piney Point."

The Sahib was shaking his head. "No. That's what Boyd

told Mildred. That's what he told everybody. The fact is Boyd took the boat out himself for a couple of weeks' cruise. He went alone."

"Alone . . ." Tom rubbed his hands over his wet hair and over his eyes and finally said, "Where did he intend to go?"

"Around Long Island. Up or down the coast. He didn't know, he intended just to cruise around and rest. Stop wherever he wanted to for fuel or groceries. Nights at any handy cove or marina. The main point was a rest for Boyd, a chance to get himself together."

"The main point was that you wanted Boyd to be alone, away from Mildred, and come to a firm decision not to sell the business," Tom said slowly.

"Maybe. Why not?"

John said, "It was a sensible plan, Tom. It just didn't work out that way. There's no way to reach Boyd tonight."

"You mean that Boyd has no alibi," Tom said slowly.

No one answered for a moment. Then John said, "Well, now he might have an alibi, Tom. He might have met somebody he knows, or somebody could have seen his boat moored somewhere."

"But we can't be sure," Tom said.

John rocked thoughtfully. "We'll let him know. In the morning he's sure to turn on his radio for the weather report. We'll get a police call for him on it. But meantime—"

"Meantime we've got to be on the safe side." The Sahib watched Tom and waited.

Tom said in a sudden burst of anger, "You ought to have told me!"

The Sahib shook his head. "I promised Boyd not to tell anybody. Especially Mildred, of course. But there we are, Tom. This is murder. The sheriff will say that either you or Boyd killed Mildred. You were found by Sister with a hammer actually in your hand. But Boyd could have been here. The sheriff knows you both. He knows that you'd cover for Boyd. I can't let you tell your story, Tom."

Tom's face was like a rock. The Sahib leaned forward, the light full on his old face and the white curls rimming his bald head. "You had a motive, Tom. Boyd had a motive. If you tell

30

your story to the sheriff it's a toss-up. You or Boyd, or both of you acting together, got rid of Mildred."

"But I didn't," Tom said as if he didn't know he was speaking.

John looked at the floor. The Sahib looked at the floor.

So both of them believed that either Tom or Boyd had killed her. They weren't sure whether it was Tom or Boyd, but they were convinced that one of them had murdered Mildred.

The Sahib said, so quietly that it was the more solemn and effective, "You or Boyd, Tom. The sheriff's known you both most of your lives. He knows how close you've been. Don't deny it, Tom," he said sharply as Tom lifted his head. "You've always covered for Boyd. Why not now?"

Tom rubbed his hands over his eyes. "You really believe that Boyd or I killed a woman. You believe that."

The Sahib's old face was lined and firm. "She's dead. Her skull's smashed in. You were there. Boyd could have been here."

"So you'd protect a murderer."

"If he's my boy, certainly." The Sahib spoke calmly and with the utmost conviction. "And if you know that you didn't kill her, Tom, then I expect you to protect Boyd as I would. Believe me, once we say it's murder it's the end of either you or Boyd, or both of you. We've got to make them believe it's an accident. If they ever get the idea that it's murder and get Sister on the witness stand, that's the end of one or the other of you. If you didn't kill her, then it's the end of Boyd. If you refuse to save yourself, save Boyd. Sister's story is as dangerous to Boyd as it is to you."

"Things are—I can't believe that Boyd—" Tom was obviously struggling with his own fear that in fact Boyd had killed Mildred. He said dully, "But marriage . . . Sister doesn't want to marry me."

Oh, don't I, I thought. But not this way. I sat down in the desk chair that squeaked. Perhaps the Sahib's preposterous plan was after all safe and sensible. Tom hadn't killed Mildred, I was sure of that, but everything that the Sahib had said was true. Once the old sheriff knew that it was murder, once he

31

got my story out of me, any jury would have to convict Tom. I remember leaning my head in my hand and thinking of Boyd—Boyd coming back to the island, Boyd waiting for a chance to meet Mildred, Boyd smashing the hammer down upon her head . . . I dropped my hands and looked up. "There were two cigarettes—I mean two people in the runabout! I saw them when I went to the big house."

I stopped, for all three men looked at me, and I suddenly felt as if I had betrayed Boyd and had told them in so many words that I had seen him. I cried, "But it wasn't Boyd! I couldn't see who it was. Besides, it was—oh, an hour at least before Tom found Mildred. And Boyd couldn't have come to the island without anyone knowing about it!"

Again I felt as if I had betrayed Boyd, for he really could have come to the island. He knew all the ways to approach secretly. The most likely way would have been for him to anchor off the east end of the island, where he knew the marshes, swim or paddle the dinghy of his cabin cruiser along one of the many inlets and walk through the pines.

Still nobody spoke, and everybody seemed to be thinking exactly what I was thinking. The Sahib said, "Are you sure that you saw two cigarettes?"

"Yes!"

The Sahib said softly after a moment, "You really would do anything to protect Tom, Sister."

I stared at him and then understood. "I wouldn't invent such a story to protect Tom. I wouldn't try to turn suspicion to Boyd in order to defend Tom. I wouldn't do that!"

The Sahib said, "Dear Sister."

I cried, "But I did see the two cigarettes. And that's not all. I saw a hammer. On the bench in the hall. Alice's pink sweater was there, too, and your newspaper, Tom. I saw a hammer when I went in."

They seemed to consider this. John said, "Was the hammer still there when you left the house?"

"I don't know. Alice's sweater was gone but—no, I can't remember the hammer."

"You'd remember if it had been there," John said shortly.

32

"Well, then Mildred took that hammer down to the boathouse herself."

The Sahib's eyelids lifted. "Of course," he said, nodding at John, "that's right. Remember, Tom, when she came to the big house after dinner she talked first about taking the Bronsons out in the old cruiser that's in the boathouse. Boyd had told her that his new little cruiser was being overhauled."

"But she couldn't have taken the Ark out. I told her that it hadn't been out in years—" Tom began.

John didn't hear him clearly. "Did you say you told her to take the Ark?"

"No. I told her she couldn't, not till it's been put in shape."

John nodded. "She was going to look at the old boat. She said that the boathouse was padlocked and she couldn't find the key. So that's exactly what she did, took the hammer down. Was it a claw hammer?" he asked Tom.

Tom shook his head. "I don't know. Yes, I think so."

"Yes," I said definitely.

"Then that's it. She intended to pry out the staples of the lock. Maybe she did. So . . ." He stopped there.

Perhaps all of us saw the same picture: Mildred with the weapon of her own murder in her hand, a swift wresting of that hammer out of her hand, a swift blow so that she had no time even to scream.

I put my hands over my eyes and then took them away again, for it only made the fancied picture more vivid.

John said, "Was the door of the boathouse open?"

I couldn't remember even looking at the boathouse. I had known that it was there and that was all. The Sahib and Tom looked at John and looked at each other. Tom shook his head. "I don't know."

The Sahib said to John, "Boyd—nobody would be such a fool as to hide in the boathouse."

Tom said, "We'd have known it, we'd have heard something. I know that Boyd wasn't there."

"Where is she now?" John asked.

The Sahib replied. "On the pier. She can't stay there all night."

"We'll see to that," John said.

Tom pounded his hand suddenly down into his fist. "I tell you I didn't kill her. And I cannot believe it was Boyd."

There was another moment of silence. Then his uncle sighed. "All right. Are you willing to take the chance that it wasn't Boyd?"

Tom looked down at his hands. I felt that he was thinking of the way he had struggled with Mildred's heavy dead body and how she had slid back into the water, under the pier, and how he'd had to drag her out and up from the sluggish black water. He wiped his hands on his coat. "No."

John said, "It may work, Sahib. If all goes well they'll call it an accident, no harm done. If there are questions, and if there's an inquiry, then we hope nobody can prove that Boyd was anywhere near the island. We hope to prove that Tom was gone before the accident, eloping with Sister. And we'll have Sister protected so they can't force her to tell anything at all. Tom will have to make up a story, something that Tom and Sister both learn by heart. Yes, it may work."

"I love both my boys," the Sahib said, and this time, too, there were no false dramatics in his manner. He waited a moment and then sat up straight and said briskly, "You've got to make the two o'clock train. Go up to the house, Tom. Get some dry clothes. Then get in to New York and down to—where, John? For a quick wedding. No waiting around to get a license. Maryland?"

"No. No, that law's been changed. Nobody can get a license in five minutes there." John chewed on his pipe. "Offhand, the only place I'm sure they could get a quick wedding is Nevada. That'll take time. But I can't be sure of nearer places. I could phone and ask somebody, but I'd better not."

The Sahib's face fell, but only for a moment. "There are planes. Easy. Let me know where to send you a wire. Only hurry. Go to the house with him, John. Be sure that nobody sees you."

But it was marriage they were arranging, my marriage to Tom, and arranging it as simply as they'd have arranged a chessboard. I said, "Tom's engaged to Alice!"

Tom gave me another long and serious look, rather as if he

had never seen me before. The Sahib said coolly, "I'll see to Alice. And there's always divorce later on when it's safe."

Tom said, "You really have no conscience, have you?"

The Sahib shrugged. "Not when your whole life and Boyd's are in danger."

Tom turned soberly to me, "You don't have to do this. You don't owe any of us anything."

The Sahib said again with deadly diplomacy, "Neither of you is obliged to do anything that goes against your will. You owe yourself something, Tom. But you owe me nothing. You owe Boyd nothing."

The Sahib never referred to his generosity in taking on the care of three children, and he never permitted any of us to refer to it. The fact that he did so now made me realize that what he asked me and Tom to do must be done. He said, "It's true that I took you in after your father was killed in that dreadful car accident and your poor mother died of her injuries a few days later. You were five or six. What else could I do? It's true that I sent for Boyd twenty-odd years ago after both his parents died in London in the last days of the buzz bombs. What else could I do? I started and built a business. You and Boyd are like my sons. I legally adopted both of you so that when the time came, as it has come, for me to retire from that business, I could hand it on to you. But you owe me nothing. I'm an old man and a sick old man. I've had a very good life. I can't ask for more for myself. You and Boyd must make your own lives." He covered his eyes with his hand.

Tom looked at him for a long moment. Finally he said, "All right. I can't refuse. But I still think it's a mistake."

John slid his stockinged foot back into his shoe and rose. "Come on, Tom."

The Sahib took his hand from his eyes and sighed.

But Tom didn't want to marry me, not even a fake marriage, assumed for a short time only, until it could be safely dissolved. I thought of a way out. "But they won't question me! Nobody knows that I saw Tom with Mildred at the pier. Nobody will ever question me." I turned to Tom. "You see? There's not another soul who knows that I could have been anywhere near the pier."

The Sahib said dryly, "Believe me, Sister, once the sheriff or anybody at all gets it into his head that Mildred was murdered, there'll be questions. Every single one of us will be questioned. Where we were, what we were doing, every possible moment will have to be accounted for. Do you think you can face the sheriff, and a court, and jury later on and lie so they'll all believe you? I don't."

I said abruptly, "Were you on the porch when I came out of the house?"

"Why, yes," the Sahib said.

"I thought so. I mean, I thought somebody was there, but I didn't know who."

The Sahib said shortly, "I saw you leave. I followed you down the steps. I came up behind you just as you—very sensibly, I must say—threw the hammer out into the water."

I said, not really intending to say it, yet curious, too, "Why did you come down the steps?"

The Sahib touched his flamboyant green scarf. "Can you possibly mean that you think I killed Mildred?"

"Why, I—why, no! That is, you couldn't have! I was ahead of you on the steps. You couldn't have passed me and reached the boathouse before I did."

Queerly, I felt exactly as if I had made too deep a dive into water that was too cold. I almost caught my breath and shook the water off my face. I went over to the Sahib. "No, you couldn't have killed her. You wouldn't have."

"I might have," the Sahib said almost pleasantly, "if it had occurred to me. And if at the same time a safe way to do it had occurred to me." But he put out a hand to me and said to Tom, "There's not much time. You'll have to get the two o'clock."

Tom gave me a look which I could not analyze except that it seemed to be reassuring, as if he'd said don't worry, I'll get this thing straightened out.

John caught the look, for as Tom opened the door he said, "Now, no funny business about this marriage, Tom. It's got to be all perfectly legal, certificate, everything. It may have to stand up under pressure and in court."

Tom didn't reply. He went out into the foggy darkness and John followed him.

The Sahib's eyes were kind, but there was also a wicked gleam in them. "You want to marry Tom. Now's your chance."

Mildred had known that, too, and had shrewdly used it as a weapon, not so much to hurt me as to stab at Tom. There had been no love lost between me and Mildred ever. Still, until that night she had never openly attacked me.

I said, "Is it so clear?"

"Tom doesn't know it. I do. Alice has a weather eye on you."

"This . . . this idea of marriage is all wrong. Tom wants to marry Alice."

He paid no attention to me. "I was very proud of you when you wrote to me after Tom's engagement and said that you wanted to use the cottage this summer, just as usual. I knew that meant that at least you intended to go down fighting. Go and change your clothes."

"There must be some other way."

The Sahib leaned forward. The wicked little gleam was gone; his eyes were dull and old and sad. "Sister, you are not old enough to know that people's whole lives can be distorted, thrown out of balance, ruined by one moment's wrong decision. This is such a moment. I can't let Tom's life, or Boyd's life, be ruined for Mildred. She wasn't worth it. You, Sister, are the keystone for Tom's safety and for Boyd's. In fact, you are our greatest source of danger. The court would have the truth out of you before you knew it, no matter how hard you tried to lie. Why did you throw that hammer out into the sea?"

I didn't answer, and he said, "Because your instinct told you that it was evidence. Do you understand what perjury really is?"

"Why, I . . . why, yes."

"You don't understand it at all. Try to see yourself under oath, swearing to tell the truth and then trying to perjure yourself. You can't do it. Go upstairs and change your clothes. You can't elope in a sweater and sneakers. Get on some city clothes. Sissy, it's for me and it's for Tom and for Boyd."

So I went upstairs. In the mirror I didn't really see myself; I had an impression of tumbled dark hair framing an utterly

37

white face. I got into the navy blue suit, cotton and cool, which I had worn to the office only that morning and thus out from town on the train, beside Tom who gave me half of his newspaper to read. It was all a dream; it was like treading water; I had no sense of progress. I forgot to change my shoes and had to go back and put on stockings and slippers. I then remembered my handbag and took it up and put a light coat over my arm.

There were voices downstairs. When I went down John was standing in the doorway saying something to the Sahib. I heard only the end of it. " . . . did it while Tom was changing clothes. Mildred had tried to get the padlock off, pried out the hasp, so it was dangling. I got the boathouse door open and lowered the dinghy."

The Sahib said coolly, "All right. It's safe for tonight, then. We'll find her in the morning."

"By the way, Leaf Trace was wandering around in the fog. I'll talk to him early tomorrow and find out whether or not he saw anything or anybody. If he did, he'll keep quiet. He owes you that, Sahib."

The Sahib nodded shortly. "I saw him scuttling across the beach. We were in the shadow of the boathouse. He didn't see us." He turned to me. "You needn't look so pale, child. You must learn that the old are very selfish, very realistic and very thick-skinned. We have to be to live so long. All right . . ." He put out his hand and I went to him. He kissed me. "Tell Tom not to forget to wire me as soon as you're married."

John went with me out into the night. The light streamed after us for a second, and then the Sahib closed the door.

Tom was waiting in the runabout. I wouldn't look at the boathouse; yet I knew that the door was closed. I thought of the water, gurgling below the little platform which ran around three sides of the boathouse, enclosing the ancient cabin cruiser and its small dinghy, where Mildred now must be lying. It seemed inhuman; it was also, as the Sahib said, realistic. John and I went out past the place where Tom had found Mildred and onto the end of the pier, which quavered a little under our footsteps. Tom put up a hand to help me down into the runabout.

John said, "Take it easy." I could see him dimly, standing on the pier above us. The light above him was still haloed with fog. Tom started the engine, which wheezed as always and was very loud. Yet I knew that the sound was blanketed by fog, and anyway there was only Leaf Trace in the big house to hear. Boyd's new house, where Alice and the two strangers, the Bronsons, were guests, seemed far away. Tom moved back away from the pier and made a wide circle; he knew the way so well that he didn't put on lights until he was out in the channel and nearing the first marker. The sound of the engine was louder when he speeded up a little. It was a strange journey, through the black fog and the black water; only the familiar old runabout itself and the familiar and exasperating cough of its engine were quite real. There were a few lights at Piney Point, but only a few. They gradually grew nearer. Tom tied up at the wharf.

The railroad station was not far from the wharf. Again I thought with incredulity of arriving only that evening on the train from the city and being met in the old runabout by Alice and Mildred. There was a light in the drugstore window. There was a light at the filling station, but the station itself was closed. There was a light at the little railroad station, but it was closed too. We met no one. Not even a dog barked. We walked to the end of the platform and there was a single light there too. Tom looked at his watch. "We barely made the train."

Dimly through the fog I could see the single light of its engine. There was a distant humming of the tracks.

Tom looked down at me. "Don't worry. We'll go into town. I'll take you to your apartment. By morning I'll have thought of some way out."

I agreed with Tom; at the same time I had the sensation of sinking, as if I were on a fast-descending elevator. "You'll think of something—" I looked out toward the island; there was no light, nothing but foggy blackness. It was as if the island and all that had happened that night had vanished forever in a limbo of blackness. "Boyd couldn't have killed her!"

"They don't know, John and the Sahib. They don't know whether it was Boyd or me."

"It wasn't you!"

"It could have been. Or Boyd could have killed her. Mildred would never have given him a divorce. She'd never have lived apart from him. She'd never have let him have his own life."

"You think it was Boyd." My words fell dully into the foggy night. The headlight of the train came nearer.

Tom replied; it was an answer, although it was indirect. "I know that I didn't kill her."

"Perhaps Boyd will have an alibi."

"It would only be the luckiest chance in the world if he had."

"You think it was Boyd," I said again.

Tom said heavily, "I don't think it was Boyd. I'm afraid of it."

"I wouldn't tell anything that would injure either of you!"

"I know. This plan for dashing off to Nevada and getting married doesn't make sense. I'll think of some other way."

The train began to slow down. It stopped, and a conductor came down from a car and waved at us. We hurried along toward him. Lights from the windows of the train shot fleetingly across our faces. I said again, "Yes, of course, you'll think of something."

The next night, very late, almost morning in fact, we arrived back in Piney Point. We had spent most of the time in traveling. The difference in time was helpful, and the sleek efficiency of plane travel between East and West coasts made it possible. Late that afternoon in the dining room of the Riverside Hotel, in Reno, Tom had duly received a message, not from his father but from John, which read only: "Thanks wire Regret inform you Mildred dead accident Sahib begs you return soonest."

We had no notion of what had occurred on the island during that time. We had been married by a justice of the peace in the Reno courthouse.

Alice and Boyd met us at the train.

.........chapter 4.....................................

Boyd saw us first and came quickly along the platform. The train gave a loud sigh and started off again.

Boyd kissed my cheek lightly. He said to Tom, "You and Sister took us by surprise."

Tom said, "We had John's wire—" He and Boyd shook hands rather as if they didn't know what else to do.

Again lights from car windows flickered over us as the train picked up speed. I couldn't see that Boyd had changed in the slightest way. Yet a murderer must somehow, very deeply and terribly, change. Boyd was exactly the same.

He and Tom resembled each other sufficiently to suggest their distant family relationship; they were both tall and to me attractive; both had gray eyes and dark hair and good strong noses and chins and foreheads. Tom, though, gave an impression of being rather square and solid and good-looking rather than handsome; Boyd was startlingly handsome in a romantic, Byronic way; yet somehow his high forehead was a trifle too narrow, his nose barely too fine, his lips just a bit too handsomely curved. He was always thin and somehow airy in his movements—wispy, I told myself.

Yet he was just the same as he had always been in his easy, affable, butterfly way.

He linked his arm through mine, and I simply could not feel that this arm and this fine, long hand on mine had wielded a hammer and struck out Mildred's life. I wondered that I had

41

no sensation of shrinking, no sensation of fear, no sensation of horror.

Alice was waiting for us at the end of the platform. The train rushed on, leaving a sudden silence behind it, and Alice came toward us, golden, long hair glistening, pink sweater over her shoulders. She put up her arms to Tom and kissed him fully on the lips.

Tom's dark head bent over her and it was a long kiss, so long that Tom began to look a little awkward, for he was now carrying a bag in each hand and Alice had both her arms around him. Boyd looked at them and looked at me and said, "The runabout's down here," as if I didn't know where it would be.

So we left Tom and Alice on the platform, still kissing for all I knew. I listened for them to come and heard myself saying, incredibly, that I was shocked to hear of Mildred's accident.

That first time I got out the word accident without tripping. Boyd, without any hesitation either, said, "Yes, it was a great shock."

Tom and Alice came behind us at last; I heard Alice's high, fluting voice, rather like a bird's when he spots a fine worm. I supposed that the Sahib and John had told her the full truth.

Even at this late hour there were furtive lights in the village. I had an odd notion that we were being watched from behind slits of barely opened curtains. Certainly everybody in Piney Point knew that we were expected and almost everybody in Piney Point had speculated upon our elopement and Mildred's death. Several dogs barked; a few loiterers near the wharf openly stared at us.

The runabout lay rocking gently in the black water. I sat beside Boyd, who took the wheel; Tom and Alice were behind us. The boat shot away from the wharf so fast that its engine spat indignantly. Tom leaned forward, near my shoulder. "We had only the wire from John. What happened?"

Boyd took one hand from the wheel and got out a cigarette. He put it in a corner of his mouth and spoke jerkily around it. "Well, that's it, really. Seems Mildred went down to the boathouse last night. It was foggy and she missed her footing there at the pier. Struck a rock, killed her instantly—or almost instantly. The doctor thinks she may have lived for a moment or two, but that she was unconscious." He fumbled for a lighter. The tiny flame lit up his fine handsome face.

There was a little pause. Then Tom said, "What doctor did you call?"

"Old Hadley, of course. Who else?"

After another pause, during which I could almost feel him choosing his words, Tom said, "They didn't have to get the coroner in on it? I mean, an inquest or anything like that?"

"Why, no. Dr. Hadley gave a certificate. Besides, he's the medical examiner."

"Oh—I'd forgotten that," Tom said.

"He said it was obviously an accident. Gave a death certificate." Boyd waited a moment and then said, "Why did you ask about an inquest?"

"I don't know. It just occurred to me."

There was another pause. Both men seemed to find difficulty in talking. The wheezing of the old engine and our rush through the water filled up the pauses. Boyd finally said, "But he did call the sheriff. At least, the sheriff came."

"What did he have to say?"

"Nothing much."

There was another pause. The lights on the island came a little nearer. Then Boyd said, "Nobody knows exactly how it happened. We have to guess. Her head—I'll give you the details later."

We knew the details; I put the picture of Mildred and the wet strands of black hair over that fearfully damaged head out of my mind, or tried to. Tom said, "When was she found?"

"The accident must have happened after you and Sister decided to elope last night. You'd have seen her if it had happened before you left. Still, you might not have. It was very foggy. She might have drifted under the pier. She was found this morning about eight. John and the Sahib had gone down to the beach and—well, found her there in the water. They called Dr. Hadley. He came right over. Said she'd been dead for hours. They sent out a radio for me—"

Tom had forgotten that he should have been surprised to see Boyd; he broke in, "But you were in London. I mean, you—"

43

Boyd took it quite in his stride; he said easily, "I knew that you were surprised to see me at the train."

Tom hadn't been surprised, and he hadn't remembered to act surprised. Neither had I. Boyd said, "No, the fact is I ducked out. I wanted to get a couple of weeks' complete rest. So I told Mildred that the cruiser needed an overhaul and took it in to Piney Point. Then instead of going to London I took out the boat. I didn't go anywhere in particular, just cruised along, fished a little, that kind of thing. Stopped for groceries and fuel when I needed them. I've got the whole itinerary all written out—"

"Written out?" Tom said sharply.

Boyd went on as if he had not sensed the alarm in Tom's question. "Last night I anchored in the cove near Marshtown. There wasn't another boat there. It just happened that way. It was so foggy you could hardly see your hand in front of you, anyway. This morning, when I got the weather report, there was a call out for me, a police call. I left the boat at the Marshtown wharf, hired a car and drove to Piney Point. That was faster than the boat."

So he didn't have an alibi, I thought; he could have come from Marshtown to the island in the night. The heavy fog was no hazard to him; instead it would have been a shield. And while there was what yachtsmen call foul water around Scatawan Island, rocks and reefs and unexpected shoals, Boyd knew a dozen ways through it.

Boyd seemed airily unconscious of the implications of what he had just said; yet the fact that he had written out his itinerary, the fact that he took the trouble to explain his actions so neatly proved that he was not at all unconscious of the need for explanation.

But Boyd would have planned a more convincing story if he had planned to kill Mildred.

On the other hand, perhaps he hadn't planned it. The hammer itself argued a frantic anger, a terrible impulse—didn't it? Boyd said calmly, "The Sahib's not too well. Doctor says he must take it easy for a few days. Another heart attack. Not a bad one—"

I couldn't be sure whether or not Boyd was adroitly turning

the subject from his lack of an alibi. I couldn't be sure either whether or not the Sahib had really had a heart attack. The Sahib could fake one if it suited his convenience.

I could almost feel Tom's reasoning, which was the same as mine. Boyd said again, "It's not a bad one, really. Don't worry about him."

Alice said in her clear musical voice, which just then had an edge to it, "Don't go so fast, Boyd. You're giving us a perfect shower bath!"

Boyd slowed down again but swirled around a buoy so quickly that the old boat rocked. Tom said in what I felt was a carefully controlled voice, "Do they know whether Mildred drowned or the blow on her head killed her?"

Boyd answered almost casually, "I guess it doesn't matter, really . . . Oh, I see what you're getting at. You mean was she conscious after she struck her head on the rocks. There's something about water in the lungs and throat. That is, the doctor—he did an autopsy—did find water in the lungs or throat or something. Anyway, he said that she must have fallen, struck her head and was unconscious but may have floated to the surface long enough to try to suck in some air. It would be automatic, he said. But then she went down again. Actually, the blow on the head killed her, but it was really a combination, the blow on the head and drowning. He couldn't say exactly which came first."

Dr. Hadley was, of course, the family doctor and had been for all the years that I could remember. The Sahib's plan, then, was working out without any question.

I was wrong. Boyd added nonchalantly, "But the sheriff asked some questions."

Tom said, too sharply, leaning over my shoulder, so I could feel the warmth of his face against mine, "What questions?"

Boyd waved one hand; it was an airy gesture, which reminded me of the Sahib at his most elusive. "Oh, this and that. Where had I spent the night? Where had I been during the week? I gave him my itinerary. Why hadn't I gone to London? Things like that. He kept asking about you too, Tom."

It seemed to me that there was the faintest touch of malice in Boyd's voice. Tom said, "What did he ask?"

45

Boyd was airy again. "When you and Sissy left. How long you'd been engaged—"

Alice made some kind of sound. It wasn't quite a laugh; it wasn't anything. Boyd went on, "How did you and Mildred get along? Questions like that."

After a pause Tom said, "I see."

The light at the boathouse loomed up like a beacon and seemed to come toward us. Above, the lights from the big house streamed out clearly.

Boyd came in so fast that I thought we were going to crash into the little pier. But we didn't, and Tom secured the boat and hauled out our two bags. Alice put up her hand and he helped her onto the pier. Boyd gave me a hand and I thought again: Can this be a murderer's hand? His grasp seemed hot, as if he had a slight fever, but that was all.

Alice looked up at Tom. "The Sahib was still awake when we left. He wants to see you."

"Of course," Tom said, "of course."

I said, "I'll go along to the cottage."

The pier shook and quavered as we trudged along it. The boathouse was a black shadow beside us. When we reached the beach Tom said, "Leave our bags here. I'll bring them to the cottage after I've seen the Sahib."

Boyd threw away his cigarette, which made a tiny red line through the darkness, and instantly lighted another. His hands shook a little and the flame wavered. Tom linked his arm through Boyd's, and the two men walked off together, arm in arm, toward the long flight of steps to the big house, so like each other in the glancing lights and shadows and so very unlike. Alice said, "I'll go with you."

So I knew that she had something to say.

She had a right to say anything she wished. We walked in silence across the strip of sand and entered the path; I knew the way, so I went first and fumbled my way through the pines and the shrubbery; there was no light in the cottage. A sharp-needled pine branch touched my forehead and I pushed it aside.

When we reached the cottage I told Alice to wait, then went ahead, across the flat stone that was its step, and opened

46

the door. There was the faint, old, woody smell that I knew. When I found the light switch the bright ceiling light disclosed the room in all its faded chintz, its sagging sofa and chairs, its comfort.

Alice came in behind me.

Somebody—Mrs. Mapping probably—had cleaned. The cups and saucers and little litter of the previous night's conference had been cleared away; the ashtrays had been emptied and the cushions plumped up. Incredibly, my brief case still stood on the table.

Alice said, "When Tom and I are married I'll have this fixed up for a guest house. It will be charming, really."

I felt myself jerk around to look at her, and then tried, too late, to grasp at calm and control. She wasn't watching me; she had gone to the kitchen door and seemed to be taking a detailed inventory of its equipment and state of repair, but I knew that she had sensed my sudden movement.

She turned in a second or two and smiled at me. The light fell strongly upon her lovely face and wide eyes and long blond hair. She wore it parted on one side and flat on top except for wide curves which fell long, below her ears, almost to her shoulders. She had a little trick of tossing back her head so that her hair swung. I had always thought of Alice as being fragile and petite; she wasn't. Her face was small, delicate as a doll's and all pink and white. Her shoulders, however, were rather broad. Under that bright light from the ceiling, there were tiny, firm bulges around her jawline. She put the left hand up to push back her hair, and her hand was broad and strong too. The diamond ring Tom had given her shone and glittered; she prolonged her little gesture of pushing back her hair so that I could see the diamond.

I was sure that the Sahib and John had told her the whole truth, the reason for what they called the elopement, everything.

They hadn't. She folded her arms and said, so flatly and loudly that for an instant she reminded me of Mildred, "I know how you managed to make Tom marry you. Mildred was right. But I've suspected it for a long time. Tom is kind and—oh, I know. I suppose it's been going on for years. All

47

this talk as if you were just a little friend of the family. You finally made Tom marry you, but it won't last. I'm still engaged to Tom and I intend to marry him. You can't stop me." She shook back her hair and walked to the door with perfect composure. She opened it, and John, on the doorstep, said, "May I come in, Sister?"

Alice pulled her sweater around those broad shoulders—and I thought it odd, even then, that I had never before noted the impression of strength she gave—and went past John without a word.

John sighed. "I hoped I'd get here before Alice talked to you—"

"You didn't explain anything to her!"

"Now, Sister—"

"What did you tell her?"

"Now, Sister—"

"Did you hear what she said?"

"No, no, I—wait a minute, Sister!"

"Do you know what she thinks? She made it perfectly clear—"

John said, "The only important thing is Tom. Isn't that right?"

I sat down. I waited a moment, and John said, "Did Boyd tell you about the death certificate?"

"Yes."

"Accident. So far that's good."

"So far?"

"Well, yes. So far. The sheriff has been asking questions."

"That's what Boyd said."

John had chosen the rocker again. He moved slowly back and forth and it gave a little murmuring squeak. "Now, of course Alice was a little upset when she heard about you and Tom. But we didn't tell her the truth simply because it's best not to tell anybody anything if you don't have to. Advice I've always given the Sahib." He eyed me mildly. "I suppose you really did go through the marriage ceremony. Everything legal, all that."

"Oh, yes."

He rocked for a moment. "I'm glad of that. I felt sure that

we could count on you. You owe so much to the Sahib. You couldn't refuse the first thing he ever asked you to do."

"I didn't."

"I was afraid that Tom was going to balk. I didn't like the look on his face when he seemed to give in."

I put my hands down flat on the table and thought of Alice's great diamond. "Oh, yes, he balked."

"He did? Then what happened?"

"I made him marry me."

"You *made* him!"

"Yes. And I suppose I've made him an enemy for life, too."

"This is for his own good—"

"I've separated him from Alice."

John pursed up his lips and looked at nothing. "But not for long. As soon as all this is fully cleared up and there's no chance of any trouble, all you have to do is get a divorce."

"You're as bad as the Sahib." I stared at my hands.

John brought his chair forward with a jerk. "Now see here, Sis, don't get an attack of conscience at this date. You went through that marriage ceremony, sure. But what of it? Plenty of people have got divorces."

"But they meant it at the time. They meant what they promised and what they swore to and . . ." I stopped.

I had meant all those promises, too. While it happened I had forgotten that it was only an expedient. I had meant everything I had sworn to.

John said, "How did you make Tom marry you?"

"Not the way Alice thinks," I said, and felt very tired. John waited, so I explained. "We took the train to town. We couldn't talk; there were other people in the car. And I kept getting more and more scared. By the time we got to New York I was terrified. I was frantic with terror. I could see myself on a witness stand, swearing that I had seen Tom—oh, well, never mind. We got to Grand Central station and Tom said he would take me to my apartment and think of some way out and let me know, and I—I wouldn't let him."

John said mildly, "What did you do?"

I thought of the echoing spaces of Grand Central, queerly empty at that hour, so that our arguing voices seemed loud. "I told him he couldn't turn Boyd over to the police. I told him that if Tom himself or Boyd was tried for murder, it would kill the Sahib. And then I said that he owed the Sahib far more than if the Sahib had been his father. As he does. And as I do. I said he had promised the Sahib, and he had. So Tom had to give in. I phoned the airport. There was a plane that stopped in Reno. There was time for both of us to go home and get some clothes and meet at the airport. I made our reservations. I wasn't at all sure that Tom would meet me at the airport. But he did."

I thought of the swift passage of the plane through the sky, with dawn flying after us, and the murky shadow of murder going with us all the way.

I thought of the steps up to the courthouse. "So we were married, and Tom sent the Sahib the wire telling him where we were. Then we walked around Reno and along the Truckee River and we were having some coffee when a boy brought Tom the wire from you. He had already looked up a flight back to New York. That's all."

It was strange that the only real moments during that hurried, dreamlike time were the moments before the justice of the peace.

He was a round, white-haired little man with rimless spectacles which glittered cheerily. His wife happened in for some reason, looked at me and at Tom in a gentle, friendly way, disappeared and returned with some roses, plucked, she told me, from her own nearby garden, and put them in my hand for a wedding bouquet. The fragrance made tears come to my eyes. The little justice of the peace was by no means imposing, but when he began the service, the power and solemnity of the words infected him with power too. I listened, and I promised what he asked me to promise and I really did forget just why we were doing all this, for I meant those promises. I had no sense whatever of making a mock of marriage or of swearing to a lie. It was as if the whole thing were real. It was real to me, even when Tom stumbled a little over my name and said, "I take thee, Sister—I mean, Cornelia—" The justice of the peace looked startled but went on, and when he said, "I now pronounce you man and wife—" I had felt that Tom was my husband and I was his wife to have and to hold—and that was wrong. Then everybody had shaken hands and Tom kissed my cheek and we went out and down the steps.

I rose. "I'm very tired, John—"

He crawled out of the rocking chair. "Of course. You can hear everything there is to hear in the morning. Not that there's much more to hear. Oh, it's all right about Leaf. He didn't see a thing. I talked to him this morning—or rather I let him talk to me. He was huddled on a rock on the south side of the island, thinking about his new book, he said. Now, after hearing about Mildred, he can't decide between having pneumonia or a nervous breakdown, so he's taking pills by the bottleful. I don't think he saw Boyd or—anybody. I cleared things up here in the cottage. Hope I did all right. The Sahib and I spent the night here; then we went out and pretended to find—"

"Yes. Boyd told us."

But he still lingered, hesitantly, as if it was hard to find words for whatever he wanted to say. His faded eyes were troubled; he touched his mustache and frowned and said, "I want you to remember, Sister, that—you see, you are in a sense a witness. I mean—" He blurted it out at last, hurriedly, "That's a dangerous position. I don't mean to frighten you but . . ."

"Why, why, Boyd wouldn't hurt me! Is that what you mean?"

"I don't know. I only—well, it's a dangerous position. Suppose Boyd saw you at the pier and thinks you know something about Mildred's murder that involves him . . ."

"But Boyd thinks I know nothing of it. He talked about the time when we left last night and—and talked about the fact that we hadn't seen Mildred. He thinks I know nothing about it."

"Then just keep him thinking that, that's all."

"John, suppose Boyd didn't kill her."

His eyes sharpened. "Did Tom tell you that *he* killed her?"

"No! No, he didn't. He couldn't have killed her. Not Tom—"

"All right. There's only one thing I want to say, Sister. You see, this kind of murder, this—you'd call it impulsive, certainly not planned, seems to indicate a moment of rage. A kind of blind striking-out at Mildred. Whoever did it has now had time to think it over. He knows what he's done. Maybe he didn't quite know it at the time it happened, but he knows it now. He's scared. He's afraid of everybody and everything and—all I wanted to say is, be careful. Goodnight, Sister."

He went away and I closed the door after him and stood leaning against it, thinking. Every word he said was true. I couldn't be afraid of Boyd, and I knew nothing at all that would make me a threat to Boyd. Yet the presence of murder, invisible, striking out of the fog, there on the island, seemed to have entered the cottage. I wished that Tom would come.

And then I thought of Alice and Tom and of my marriage which wasn't a marriage at all but still to me felt like marriage.

Yet in cold fact I had forced Tom to marry me; I had worked on his love and loyalty for the Sahib and for Boyd; I had done everything a woman can do. But I hadn't made him marry me in the way Alice had not very subtly implied; just then it seemed rather a pity that Alice was wrong.

I went upstairs and turned on the light in the bedroom. John hadn't cleared up here. My old denim skirt and sweater were flung over a chair exactly as I had left them. My sneakers lay under the dressing table. On the dressing table, shining in the light, lay a hammer.

52

.........chapter 5.............................

It was the same hammer.

It couldn't be the same hammer. It was outside the realm of possibility that the hammer which had killed Mildred, the hammer I had taken from Tom's hand and thrown out into the sound, could have returned.

Presently the little room, the white curtains, the old rag rug stopped spinning around me. I went over to the hammer and looked down at it. It was large. It was a claw hammer. It seemed to me that the wooden handle was water-soaked. After a long time I touched it and it wasn't water-soaked at all.

So of course it wasn't the same hammer. It could not possibly be the same hammer. But it was a hammer and Mildred had been killed by a hammer and I had thrown that hammer out into the water and darkness.

So why was a hammer lying there on my dressing table? It was horribly incongruous, nudging a little pocket comb in a gold case which the Sahib had once given me for Christmas, and a red chiffon scarf and a tiny bottle of an expensive perfume which I had purchased for myself. Nobody had any use for a hammer, not in that room.

Or had somebody a use for it?

It was only then that I seemed to hear John's words. He had said that I was a witness and that I might be in danger because a witness to a murder was in a dangerous position and that whoever murdered Mildred might think I had seen too much.

But Boyd wouldn't hurt me. Besides, I had not seen Boyd; I had only seen Tom bending over Mildred, trying to pull up her body, holding the hammer in his hand.

But not that hammer.

I had seen two cigarettes in the runabout. The Sahib had all but said that I had invented the two cigarettes, hoping to suggest that Boyd had in fact been in the runabout. Neither Tom nor John had seemed much interested in the two cigarettes, and the fact was that I had seen them almost an hour before Mildred had been found. So whoever sat there, idling and smoking, could have gone long before she was killed. And only John or the man who wanted to buy the business, Bronson—or even his wife, or Leaf Trace, or Boyd—could have been in the runabout at that time.

But if Boyd was there, then who was with him? John, or Leaf? Or one of the Bronsons?

The two cigarettes were, in fact, evidence of exactly nothing except—just perhaps—Boyd's presence. One cigarette might have suggested somebody sitting in the runabout, waiting for Mildred. Two cigarettes only suggested two people and a conversation which so far nobody had admitted, and since there was no police investigation, no questions about it could be asked. It struck me, then, too, that there was a space of time between Mildred's departure from the big house and her murder. Not much time, perhaps; I thought about half an hour. But I wondered what she had done and where she had been during that time. Again, since there was no police investigation and since she was dead, there was no way to make very satisfactory inquiry about that.

There must be some perfectly sensible, practical reason for that hammer having been left on the dressing table.

It had an ugly cold gleam from the lights.

I began to think more clearly. I had jumped to the conclusion that some way, somehow, the hammer was a threat to me. There was no reason at all to believe that even for an instant. If anyone was afraid that I had seen too much, he wouldn't merely leave a hammer somewhere around, in the cottage, on my dressing table. There was nothing to be gained by that. Anybody who was afraid of me would take some positive action. In other words, he'd try to kill, not merely suggest killing.

That was not exactly a cheering reflection either; I thrust it away. I began to feel like a fool for having permitted my thoughts to fly off into such fantastic and unreasonable surmises. It was only a matter of association. A hammer had killed Mildred, and probably for the rest of my life the mere sight of a hammer would induce ugly fancies.

In the morning I would ask Mrs. Mapping if she had left it there. No, I wouldn't; the next day was Sunday—indeed, it was already Sunday. Mrs. Mapping and her daughter never came to the island on Sunday. I'd have to wait until Monday. It wasn't important.

The cottage was so quiet that when I opened the dormer window beside the bed I thought that I could hear the slow lap of waves down near the boathouse where the old runabout was now tied as usual.

I wished that there had been more chance for me and Tom to talk. We had been together during that long flight westward and long flight eastward again; yet always there had been people around us, within hearing distance. And always there had been a kind of nightmare circle of strangeness; murder had entered our lives. On the way back I slept some, but not enough. I remembered the pretty stewardess giving us dinner and Tom smoking one cigarette after the other.

It might be weeks, it might be months before we could be sure that Mildred's death was accepted as an accident. Alice would not like waiting long for my divorce from Tom.

I got out of my wrinkled suit, showered, went to bed and listened for the opening of the cottage door and for Tom's footsteps in the room below. But I didn't hear anything, and it was full morning light when Tom called to me and said coffee was ready.

Sun was pouring in through the windows. It was warm, almost too warm and balmy. I knew the island and its moods; the warmth and the sunniness were deceptive. I got into a clean denim skirt and fresh white shirt, and it seemed only a few moments since I'd shucked myself out of island clothes on the night of Mildred's murder and got into the suit which now hung in the closet, to go to the city, to soar through the sky ahead of the dawn, to marry Tom, and come back again.

When I came down the stairs Tom slid toast onto a plate. He looked perfectly natural and everyday in his faded jeans and scuffed loafers, with his hair still wet from the shower which I hadn't heard at all. He had slept on the sofa; the cushions were all plumped up again but there was a neat little stack of blankets and a pillow on a chair. We hadn't discussed any means and ways of convincing anybody that our marriage was a real marriage—which legally it was. It hadn't required discussion. The Sahib and John knew the facts; only Alice might have expected me to take up residence in the big house—Alice and the two strangers, the Bronsons. Leaf Trace was too much preoccupied with himself to take much interest in anybody else.

But of course the sheriff must be satisfied about the validity of our marriage. Tom sat down, and I drank some of the hot coffee and said over the cup, prosaically, "It's going to storm."

Tom nodded. "Smells like it. I've talked to Boyd. I'm not so sure now that he killed Mildred."

"I know. I felt that last night, too. But Boyd was always a good actor."

"Well—yes. But Boyd never has lied to me. He knows I'll stand by him."

"Murder is different."

"But he must guess that we've done everything we can to shield him! He's too smart not to wonder just how it happened that you and I shot off to Reno and Mildred wasn't found until morning and—"

"Did you tell him why?"

"No. If he killed her, he had provocation. Oh, I'm not excusing Boyd. But he—I—"

I said slowly, "If Boyd didn't kill her, then who—"

Tom broke in. "That's what I've been thinking ever since it happened. I asked Boyd directly. He laughed a little and said that he'd expected everybody to ask him that. But he said again that he hadn't been near the island."

"He doesn't have an alibi."

56

"Oh, that's been fixed," Tom said a little grimly. "The Sahib told me. John made some excuse to go to New York yesterday. Actually he went to Marshtown. One of the men in the company shipping room has a summer cottage there. He's worked for the company for nearly thirty years. John has got him primed. If it's necessary he'll say that he saw Boyd and Boyd's boat in the Marshtown cove that night, but that Boyd didn't see him."

I thought that over for a moment. "Did Boyd know that last night? I mean, when we were talking, coming back to the island?"

Tom looked uncomfortable. "Well, yes, he did. But he says there's time enough to let the sheriff himself dig out the alibi. If it comes to that. John says so, too."

"They seem to have covered everything, Boyd's alibi, our marriage—"

"Oh." Tom dug into his pocket. "Here. I felt like a fool yesterday when the justice of the peace asked for the ring. I hadn't thought of it. This was my mother's. The Sahib kept it for me. I got it out of the safe at the big house last night. See if it fits."

He put the gold band on my finger. It was a little large, but it gleamed softly on my hand. It was far lovelier in its way than Alice's diamond engagement ring. But of course it wasn't real, not for me. It wasn't real, but I closed my hand around it.

Tom said, "Get some thread or something and wind it around so that it won't slip off."

"All right." He might have been telling me to gather up some fishing tackle or help him tie up a boat.

"The sheriff phoned early this morning. He'd heard that we got back last night. Said he'd like to talk to us."

I must have looked terrified, for he added, "Don't let it bother you. Just stick to the story we agreed upon. You're not afraid of him, are you?"

The sheriff was a familiar figure to us all. So I lied to Tom and said that I was not afraid, thought of the lies I was prepared to tell the sheriff and hoped that I wouldn't show by so much as the flicker of an eyelash that I was lying. It would

57

certainly be far easier to lie to the sheriff than to a jury and a prosecuting attorney.

I said, "Is the Sahib all right?"

"Oh, yes. He wouldn't admit faking a heart attack, of course, not even to me, but I think he is."

"He still thinks Boyd killed her?"

Tom rose. "He's still not sure whether I did it or Boyd did it."

"But you've *told* him you didn't!"

"And Boyd said he didn't. My uncle would like to believe both of us. He can't. Oh, I don't know! Perhaps Boyd was lying to me. You see, it was the kind of murder that Boyd could have been goaded into. It had to be done in a moment of ungovernable anger, a moment really of something like frenzy."

"Tom!" It seemed unbelievable, but I had forgotten the hammer on my dressing table. "Somebody left a hammer—it's not important, of course. Mrs. Mapping must have left it there, but—"

Tom leaned over and caught my wrists in his hands. His face was all at once older and very white. "What are you talking about?"

I told him quickly. "But it wasn't the same hammer—"

"It couldn't have been." His face was still white, though. He dropped my wrists and went up the little stairway, three steps at a time. I heard him in my room, crossing the floor. In a moment he called down to me. "Where is it?"

I ran up the stairs after Tom and we looked everywhere. It was not on the dressing table. It was not on the window seat. It was not anywhere. There was simply no hammer.

"But nobody came in last night," I said. "I'd have heard it."

"No, you wouldn't. I called to you when I came in and you were sound asleep. I even came upstairs and looked in the door and you didn't hear me. Anybody could have come in and taken that hammer away before I came to the cottage last night, and you'd never have known it."

"It couldn't have been Boyd. You were with him at the big house—"

"Not all the time. He left me to talk to the Sahib. After

we'd talked awhile I opened the safe in the Sahib's room and had to rummage through a lot of things, rubbish for the most part, before I could find the ring. No, Boyd had time to come down here and take the hammer. You're sure you didn't dream it?"

"I touched it."

"*Why—*"

"I don't know. Yes, I do. I had a queer notion that it might be water-logged—"

Tom gave a kind of exclamation and put his arm around my shoulder. "Things can't come back from the sea."

I rubbed my cheek a little against his arm, which was warm and comforting. Tom said with sudden anger in his voice, "I wish Mildred had floated out to sea and never come back."

"No, you don't. We'd never have known—"

"It's better not to know than to think of Boyd as—" He withdrew his arm and looked down at me in a puzzled way. "Yet this hammer business—I mean, leaving a hammer here in your room and then creeping in and taking it away again— doesn't seem like Boyd . . ." He stopped. It did seem like Boyd. It seemed like the kind of senselessly illogical thing that Boyd might do merely in order to threaten me. It was as if Boyd—or someone—had said to me: Be careful; if you think you know more than is good for you, keep your mouth shut. It was like a dreadful reminder: Remember what happened to Mildred.

Tom was following the same line of reasoning. He said, "Sister, have you told us every single thing you saw or—or heard —or somehow knew about that night?"

"Yes. Oh, yes."

"This hammer—well, it seems like a threat. A kind of warning to you. As if it was meant to remind you of what happened to Mildred."

"There isn't anything else I know."

"You're sure? It could be some very small thing."

"I'm sure, Tom."

He looked searchingly down into my face and then out the window toward the too sunny, too warm, too balmy day. From the window we could see only blue sky and green pines.

59

Finally he spoke, with long pauses between sentences as if he were making a record which must be exact and firm. "When you went into the hell room that night, Alice left. Mildred left, too. I didn't see either of them pass the bench in the hall. I didn't see anybody else in the hall. I don't remember seeing a hammer on the bench at all. I was angry, I was furious. I waited till I was sure that Mildred had gone. I thought she'd gone home."

He paused for a long time and then went on. "I knew you were working in the hell room. I went out to the porch and sat for a while with the Sahib. He said Mildred had gone down to the beach; I remember saying that I supposed she was looking at the padlock. Neither of us thought much of that. He'd heard everything that Mildred had said. Finally, after—oh, it must have been thirty minutes or so, I was sure that Mildred had taken the path around to their house and gone home. I went down the steps. No reason; I was on edge. I stopped at the first landing and smoked. I didn't hear anybody on the beach. All that time, on the porch and on the landing, I didn't hear voices, I didn't hear anything. Of course, I wouldn't unless she had screamed; it's too far and there was the fog. Just for something to do after a while I went on down, slowly, taking my time, not thinking of anything but Mildred and her determination to get Boyd to sell the business."

Here he waited a moment and took a long breath. "When I came out on the beach I heard a noise—sounded like thumps against the pier or something. I crossed to the boathouse, mainly out of idle curiosity. But then—then I saw Mildred in the water. Her face and . . . anyway, I tried to haul her up and almost had her on the pier when she slid back into the water. And then you were there. You took the hammer. I'd picked it up—my foot struck it—I didn't realize that I had it in my hand until you took it and threw it away. It all happened so fast—"

"Tom, do you think that Mildred's murderer was there, somewhere, close?"

"I think whoever killed her got away as fast as he could. But she may have been struck some time before she died, you know. She must have been unconscious but—still struggling perhaps. Oh, I don't know! And we'll never know till we get the police—"

Boyd called from downstairs. "Tom?"

There was a moment while we stood there, perfectly still, looking out over the green pines. Even Boyd's voice, so usual, so natural, seemed to refute the dreadful accusation of murder. Then we turned, together, and started down the stairs. The stairway was so narrow that I went first; Boyd was standing in the doorway shutting out the sunlight, smiling a little. "Good morning, Sissy. Do you mind if I take Tom with me today? It's the services for Mildred, you know. At her home up in Charlesburg. They sent the—that is, they sent her from Piney Point by the night train. You'll come with me, won't you, Tom?"

Boyd was already dressed to leave; he wore a handsome suit of dark Italian silk, a white shirt and black tie; he carried a raincoat over his arm. He looked very handsome and perfectly natural. Tom made some kind of movement in which Boyd seemed to sense negation, for he looked at Tom. "Please come. I can't face it alone. We'll be back by night."

"Oh, you chartered a plane then," Tom said.

"Sure. The pilot is waiting now, I suppose. We'll go to Piney Point and then take a car to the airport. It won't take long. We'll be back by seven at the latest, more likely earlier. Please, Tom—"

"I don't think so," Tom said slowly. But I knew that it was hard for him to resist Boyd. I also knew that somebody in the family ought to accompany Boyd. I said after a moment, "We'll both go."

Boyd thanked me with another of his charming and dreadfully appealing smiles, "Darling Sissy, how very like you. But you can't go with us, dear. The plane's too small. Now how about it, Tom?"

By then Tom had had time to come to my conclusion. "All right," he said. "But we've got to be back here by seven."

"Heaven knows I don't want to hang around that place. Have you got some coffee, Sissy?" Boyd asked.

Tom dragged out his bag from where it stood behind the sofa, and carried it upstairs. I gave Boyd coffee; we could hear

61

Tom in my room above, slinging things around. He came down, dressed in a darkish business suit.

I said, "I'll take you over to Piney Point and bring the boat back."

"Oh, don't bother," Boyd said pleasantly, "Alice is taking us. She's in the boat now, waiting for us. Thanks all the same, Sissy. See you." He waved with all the insouciance and charm in the world, and Tom frowned after him as he disappeared along the path.

"Overdoing it," he said. "He's scared. Do you really not mind this? I mean—well, that hammer—"

"If Boyd put it there and then crept into the cottage last night while I was asleep and took it away, then I'm perfectly safe. He'll not be here at all today. You'll be with him. And somebody must go. It'd better be you."

Boyd wasn't going to let Tom have any second thoughts. He called back, "Hurry up, Tom—"

Tom still hesitated, frowning; then he bent over, gave me the kind of kiss that he'd given me on Christmas or my birthday for many years, seemed to try to think of something he wanted to say and ended up with, "You'd better see the Sahib. Stay at the big house all day. Then things will be all right—"

"Yes," I said.

So he went off down the path, and presently I followed. I was in time to hear the wheezy old engine of the runabout start up and in time to see them leave. Tom was sitting beside Alice, who was at the wheel, her long golden hair streaming back. I turned back to the cottage but still listened, so that I heard the beat of the engine suddenly mingled with the more regular and efficient beat of another engine. Apparently the two boats had met; the engines of both seemed to idle for a moment; then the runabout resumed its wheezy way and the second boat came nearer. I turned and went back to the beach.

The runabout was plunging along toward Piney Point, casting back two white wakes. The second boat was already being tied at the pier by the sheriff.

He rose, squinted through the sunlight and saw me. "Sissy," he called, "I want to talk to you."

.........chapter 6...........................

I didn't want to talk to him, He had always been a kind and fatherly sort of friend to me and Boyd and Tom. Once when the engine of the old runabout had conked out and we found ourselves out in a foggy night, cold and hungry and scared—although Boyd and Tom and perhaps all three of us tried to hide our scare—a Coast Guard boat had come out of the darkness. The Sahib had told the sheriff that we were still out; the sheriff found us, plucked us into the Coast Guard boat, wrapped me in his coat and took us back to the island, towing the runabout.

His name was Cable and everybody called him Sheriff, nothing else; he was tall, rangy and brown the year around, and showed every wrinkle and line of his sixty-odd years. He took my hand and wished me happiness, and his light blue eyes were so keen and searching that I felt a dreadful discomfort. I asked him into the cottage, and he came in and lit a cigarette. I thought of the two cigarettes in the runabout just before Mildred was murdered and told myself to be very careful. I must not mention the two cigarettes, which would suggest Boyd's presence; I must not deviate in the slightest way from the story which Tom and I had invented together and which I had memorized. It would have been easier if Tom had been there to tell it.

The sheriff settled back. "I met Tom and Boyd."

"Yes. Tom is going with Boyd to services for Mildred. Somebody had to go, of course—"

63

He nodded, watching me. "Seems too bad. A thing like this the very night you and Tom—" He drew a long breath on the cigarette and said, "eloped. How long had you planned to elope?"

"Not very long. In fact, only that night."

"Yes," he said, "seems too bad. You had all the time in the world to make up your minds to get married. How'd it happen you went way off to Reno like that, so quickly? Seems like the Sahib would have wanted a big wedding. Seems like you'd have wanted it, Sissy. Girls do."

This time I spoke the truth. "I didn't care what kind of wedding. Besides it was a—a nice wedding." I tried to think of something convincing. "I had a bouquet, roses."

He nodded again; his hair was perfectly white and very thick above his tanned face. "Sure. You've always liked Tom."

He said it simply and honestly, but I could feel myself flush a little as I wondered how and when I had made it so very evident, apparently to everyone but Tom, that I wanted to marry him. He added, "But then this young woman—Alice, is it?"

"Alice Warren."

"Warren, yes. Well, then she came along last winter—a friend of Mildred's, wasn't she?"

"They were friends, yes. Alice has been staying here since she and Tom—I mean—"

"Since their engagement," the sheriff said. "Everybody in Piney Point knew about the engagement. The womenfolk read it in the papers. That was the girl at the wheel when I met them just now. Bright yellow hair—"

"Yes—"

"Stunning," he said, watching me. "But here you and Tom go flying off in the middle of the night clear across the country, without a word to anybody. Not even a word to Alice. I hear she was very upset when she heard about it." I may have looked questioning, for he said, "Henrietta Mapping told me."

Henrietta was Mrs. Mapping's daughter; she would have told him with dramatic relish. Henrietta's beady black eyes and sharp ears must have outdone themselves that day. The sheriff shook his head. "That wasn't the thing to do, Sissy."

"No—that is—well, no, but—"

"But what?"

"Well, you see—" I hastily assembled the bits and pieces of the story Tom and I had agreed upon. "Well, you see, it happened this way." I took a breath and began. "I went up to the big house that night to get some work. Tom's brief case and mine had got mixed up in the boat coming from Piney Point—"

"You came on the late train," the sheriff said quietly, but showing that he had asked questions.

"Yes, we were held up at the office and missed the early one. We got to Piney Point at close to eight—"

"Seven fifty-four," the sheriff said.

"Yes. Alice and Mildred met us in the runabout. I came here and Tom went to the big house. It was about eleven when I discovered that I had Tom's brief case instead of my own. So I went up to the big house, and Tom and the Sahib and Mildred and Alice were all there. I went into the hell—I mean the study and worked there on some notes Tom had made. Then I came back to the cottage."

Up to that point it was clear sailing. Now I had to watch each word. "I met Tom and he walked along with me and we began to talk and—well, we'd talked of marriage before, of course, and had—" Lies really do stick in your throat; I coughed a little and went on. "We had intended to marry, you see. But then Alice— Well, anyway, it just seemed simpler and better all around if we went to—to Reno and were married and explained later. So we did."

The sheriff smoked and thought. "Well, I guess you knew what you wanted to do. Seems as if you'd have told this girl though, this Alice. When did you last see Mildred?"

His question sliced smoothly and neatly into the web of my lies. "I saw her at the big house. They said she was found near the boathouse—"

He nodded and waited. I said, "We took the runabout to Piney Point. It was very dark and foggy."

"You mean you didn't see Mildred when you left."

"Was she dead then?"

"Maybe. The doctor can't say exactly. Of course, if you'd seen her you'd have tried to do something for her."

I said, "Of course." I wondered how much longer I could lie, and reminded myself that it was Tom's whole future for which I was lying.

The sheriff said in a conversational way, "That wound on her head. Doc Hadley says it was rocks she struck. Must have been. Still, I've been around this coastline most of my life. I don't know that I ever saw head wounds just like that." He put out his cigarette. "Actually, it looked to me more like, say, a hammer than rocks.'

I'm sure that I didn't make a sound. I'm sure because my breath stopped and my heart stopped too.

The sheriff waited, giving me a chance to speak. My heart finally started with a dreadful jump and thudded and I was afraid he would hear; I looked hard at the rug so he couldn't see any change at all in my eyes. He said presently, "Now of course I wouldn't want to give the impression that I think maybe somebody hit her on the head with a hammer and she fell into the water and died there. That would be a bad thing to suggest—unless I had some proof of it. Why, folks might think that Boyd and Tom got together and got rid of her like that."

"Oh, no!"

The sheriff watched me with those clear eyes. I walked over to the table and waited a second; then I turned to look at him again. "Sheriff, they said it was an accident. Now you are talking about murder!"

"No, now, Sissy, wait a minute. I've got to explore possibilities. If something seems to me a little peculiar, not quite what I'd expect, I've got to ask questions. Haven't I?"

"Tom and Boyd wouldn't have conspired together and killed Mildred! That's a dreadful accusation to make."

"I didn't make any accusation. I was just thinking of those two, Tom and Boyd. Tom would do anything to help Boyd out of any kind of trouble he'd got himself into. Always did. Not that Tom was any more or less of a hell-raiser when he was a kid than any other kid. Neither of them—" He paused and ruffled up his thick white hair and seemed to think back. "No, I can't say either of them got into any very serious mischief-making. But the way I've got it figured, Tom always

66

sees to Boyd. I'm not sure that Boyd would put himself out much to help Tom."

"Tom wouldn't murder—anybody—"

"He'd have been very thankful if Boyd could have got rid of Mildred. Seems to me—well, there's divorce."

I thought first about the false kind of marriage I had undertaken, with both eyes open. Then I realized that the sheriff was talking about Mildred and Boyd. "I don't think there was ever any question of divorce. If there was, I never knew it."

"Seems to me Mildred wasn't the kind of woman to be put off that way. Besides—" He paused to think again, his tanned face very grave. "Besides," he said suddenly, "if this was murder—now, don't fly at me, Sissy, I'm saying *if*—if this was murder, looks to me more like a murder of impulse. Nothing thought out ahead of time. Of course, that kind of murder is hard to track down and prove. But if anybody hit her on the head with a jagged rock or—"

"You said a hammer," I said with a curious boldness, facing him.

He nodded without any change in his eyes. "Or a hammer. Seems to me that all of it could have happened just as it did. If Boyd or Tom got good and mad and hauled off and hit her with a hammer, it would be consistent with the facts as we know them. But Tom and Boyd would stick up for each other. Did that happen?"

"No!" I almost shouted it and then realized that I was denying too vigorously. I said, "Boyd wasn't here—"

"He could have got here."

"It couldn't have been Tom because he was with me." I said, again with a pretense of boldness and courage which I did not at all possess, "Do you really believe she was murdered? Are you accusing Boyd or Tom—"

"My goodness, Sissy, don't fly off the handle like that." He rose and went to the door. He turned, put up his brown old hand, which was exceedingly muscular in spite of his age, as if to suggest my silence and said, "You see, this sudden wedding sounds kind of remarkable to me. Yes, remarkable. You could have got married any old time. No special reason for eloping the night Mildred died. So—I thought to myself, I thought, just suppose Boyd or Tom had something to do with Mildred's death, just suppose it wasn't accident, just suppose Sissy knows something about it . . . Well, I did think, Sissy, that a real quick marriage to Tom might be a very good way to keep you from telling anybody—me, for instance—exactly what happened. If you're married to Tom you can't be forced to give evidence; anybody would know that. Didn't take much thinking on my part. But then of course I've known all three of you a long time. Known the Sahib too. Yes, I've known the Sahib. I may be wrong; I hope I'm wrong. But the whole thing looks a little fishy to me. I'll see you later, Sissy."

He went out the door and I sat down on the sofa and wished that Tom were there. I wished I had not gone to the big house the night Mildred was murdered.

It seemed to me that long friendship and knowledge lay behind the sheriff's altogether too accurate guesses. He was nobody's fool.

And he knew us far too well. He was a dedicated reader; he had said, smiling, that he kept the job of sheriff because there was so little crime in Piney Point that he had time to read. He and the Sahib had long discussions and sometimes arguments about books, and downright battles over their chess games in the long summer evenings on the island.

I knew Mr. Cable far too well, too. He was like the rocks of Scatawan Island; nothing could move him. It would be perfectly useless for me or Tom or Boyd or the Sahib to appeal to him, to try to lull what were obvious and altogether too accurate suspicions. He often won when he played chess with the Sahib. I wondered now how the Sahib could have believed that the sheriff would not shrewdly suspect every move we had made.

But suspicion was not proof, I told myself. Perhaps it was then that I began to see that we had to know for certain whether or not Boyd had killed Mildred.

I rose and went to the door, aware that something had changed, and I saw that the storm which the unusually balmy and still morning had predicted was now coming. The sun had gone; there were no more dappled lights and shadows along the path. Everything looked a peculiarly vivid green.

My wedding ring nearly slid off my finger, so I went up to my bedroom and wound white thread in and out around it, in a close little hump for the inside of my finger. Tom's clothes were strewn about, slacks over a chair, shirt on the floor, loafers under the dressing-table bench.

Somebody, a man, called from downstairs, in a mellow, warm voice, "Mrs. Esseven—" He called, "Mrs. Esseven—" again before it occurred to me that he was addressing me. I broke off the thread, put the ring on my finger, where it now fit snugly, and went to the little flight of stairs. I could see him then, and I knew that he must be the mysterious, elusive, yet oddly ubiquitous Mr. Bronson, who looked like a tailor's dream. He also looked rather feral, as if he would be far more comfortable walking around on four legs than on two. He wore pale blue slacks and a pale blue shirt with a monogram on the pocket; he was fat and rosy and his eyebrows angled up from the bridge of his nose in a way which was exactly like a tiger's scowl. He smiled warmly, too warmly. "Is this the bride? I have to introduce myself. I'm George Bronson."

So of course I came downstairs and said how do you do and wondered what zoo he had escaped from and how, which was odd, for he was remarkably polite and pink and clean and bald. Flashing very large white teeth which rather suggested that he had eaten his keeper, he said that he didn't wish to intrude but that he had seen the sheriff's boat tied at the pier and wanted to talk to him.

"I understand that he is a friend of the family," he said, smiling and showing those dangerous teeth.

I said yes, and Mr. Bronson said, "You see—well, the fact is of course, that we, my wife Nadine and I, wish to leave."

I felt that I'd like him to leave, the sooner the better. I said that of course I understood.

"My wife Nadine was devoted to poor Mildred. This is very distressing to her. However, there's a little problem. Yesterday the sheriff asked us to stay on at the island for a few days. He didn't say how long. And he didn't say why he wanted us to stay here."

So as soon as he knew of it the sheriff had thought, as he said, that there was something fishy about Mildred's death. I said that I didn't know anything about it and that I supposed the sheriff had gone to the big house to see the Sahib.

Mr. Bronson looked me up and down; I thought that a faint gleam of approval came into his eyes, rather as if the tiger had glimpsed a more or less toothsome tidbit but wasn't really hungry at the moment. "Well, then, I'll not intrude. May I wish you and Tom every happiness. I've not seen Tom this morning. I understand that he went with poor Boyd on his tragic errand."

I nodded. Mr. Bronson lingered a moment, finally said in a rather disgruntled way that it was about to rain, and left. As he went down the path, the first few big drops were splashing down on his beautiful blue shirt and slacks, and it gave me a little satisfaction to see him begin to hurry, although he didn't actually drop down on all fours.

I wondered why Mr. Bronson wanted to buy a publishing company; I wondered where he had come from if not a zoo, which did seem a little improbable, and where he'd got the money with which to buy the company. But Mildred had been determined to sell it to him; they were in obvious agreement, which presented no motive for murder on Bronson's part. It seemed to me rather a pity that such a likely-seeming candidate for murderer would reasonably have to be eliminated.

Drops began to drum upon the roof and I hurried to close the windows. The rain made such a din that I felt shut off and alone. I hoped that the storm had not delayed the departure of the plane which Boyd had chartered.

Darkness seemed to seep out of the corners and down the stairway, and the rain thudded down as if it had a kind of special animosity and wished to blot out the cottage and the island itself. The corners of the living room were obscured; the kitchen became shadowy space and the little open stairway seemed curtained in darkness. Anybody could come down the stairs or out from the kitchen in that din and dusk without my knowledge.

Of course there was nobody to come down the stairs or out of the kitchen. Nevertheless I turned on lights, so that everything leaped out of the dusk and became domestic and accustomed. The rain pounded on the roof. I didn't hear John when he knocked; as he opened the door I was standing at the table. I caught the flicker of motion and stopped a scream on my lips when I saw his pink and wrinkled face peering in.

I suppose I told him to come in. He couldn't have heard me for the noise of the rain. He came in and shut the door and shook himself out of his raincoat. "I'm sorry, I didn't mean to frighten you. I knocked."

"I didn't hear. The rain is so loud. I'll take your coat."

"Never mind." He hung it over a chair, where it dripped on the floor.

"How is the Sahib?"

"Oh, he's all right. Asleep when I left the big house."

I sat down, and John took the rocking chair to which he had established something like squatter's rights.

He said, rocking, that he had seen Tom and Boyd leave. "I was on the porch at the big house. Glad Tom went with Boyd. Looks better."

"I didn't hear Alice come back from Piney Point."

"Oh, yes, she came right back. The sheriff came up to the big house and talked to the Sahib and me for a while. Then he talked to the Bronsons and to Leaf. I'm afraid—in fact, it's obvious that the sheriff is not satisfied that it was an accident."

"We didn't deceive him for a moment! He guesses why Tom and I married, and he thinks I know something of Mildred's murder."

"I was afraid we couldn't pull any wool over his eyes. But he only guesses, Sissy. He doesn't know. He has no proof. There's a difference."

"He's very close to the truth." I locked my hands together; the wedding ring shone under the lamp light. "Tom is not so sure now that it was Boyd."

"Huh?" John cupped his hand at his ear. We had both been shouting over the din of the rain.

I repeated it more loudly. "I said Tom is not so sure now that it was Boyd."

"Oh. Why not?"

"Boyd says he didn't kill her."

John rocked for a moment, got out cigarettes, put the package back in the sagging pocket of his worn tweed coat and pulled his pipe from another pocket. "But he wouldn't admit it, would he?" he said, hunting for his tobacco pouch. He added, almost casually, "And neither would Tom admit it."

"But Tom didn't!" I cried.

John said, "Dear Sissy," in an indulgent way which was infuriating. It was also a little frightening. John found the pouch, carefully filled his pipe and said, "Do you mind my pipe?"

I shook my head and tossed a book of matches toward him, rather hoping it would hit him. But he caught it dextrously as I said, "It was *not Tom.*"

John either did not hear me distinctly or chose not to reply directly. He said, "If Boyd's got any sense, and he has, he wouldn't admit it to anybody."

"I'm not so sure now myself."

"Huh?" John said again. "Sorry, I seem to be getting a little deaf."

He'd been getting a little deaf for years. I shouted, "I said that I'm not so sure now myself that Boyd killed her. I keep thinking of those two cigarettes in the runabout."

John made a silencing motion with his hand, shot out of the rocking chair, which tipped wildly backward, and flung open the door. Rain and wind hurled into the room. John shut the door and turned to me. "I thought I heard somebody at the door. We're talking too loud. I wouldn't want anybody to overhear."

"Nobody's out in that rain listening. He'd be drowned by now."

"Mildred *was* drowned of course."

"No, I didn't mean that—" I stopped because this time I heard the fusillade of knocks on the door. I hurried to open the door, and a gust of wind and rain and a woman came in.

She looked drenched to the skin; her hair hung wildly over her face. I knew it must be Nadine Bronson before John got the door shut and introduced us. "Sissy, this is Mrs. Bronson. This is Tom's wife, Mrs. Bronson. Dear me, you did get wet, didn't you," he said mildly.

Mrs. Bronson uttered a kind of strangled sound, pushed back her mop of reddish hair, which showed dark at the roots, and

72

eyed me with a vivid, sparkling green gaze. She looked at that moment as if she might spit, like a wet cat. My impression of the Bronson family seemed thoroughly confused with the animal world. She said, "So you're the bride. How do you do? All I can say is you'd better avoid Alice on a dark night. I'd thank you for the loan of dry clothes."

.... chapter 7 ....

John said he'd better leave. Mrs. Bronson didn't even look at him, and he trudged out to the kitchen and gathered up his raincoat. Rather taken aback by her greeting, I said that of course she could have something dry and invited her upstairs.

"I'm a size fourteen," Mrs. Bronson said and eyed me. "Bigger than you, I'm afraid. Still, I'm wet as a drowned rat."

More of the animal kingdom, I thought fantastically and led the way upstairs. John shouted back something as he left. He closed the door hard behind him, and Nadine said, "I've never been in the cottage. I've been here only since Friday noon. Seems like years. How long are they going to keep us here?"

I said that I didn't know. The rain was louder, if possible, when we got up to my bedroom. She glanced around her, and her green eyes rested for a reflective moment on Tom's hastily flung-down clothes, which did indeed look domestic, and I wished briefly and meanly that Alice could see them. Nadine's mouth was rather narrow, but now that her hair was off her face I could see that she was handsome, thin and, I thought, sophisticated in the extreme. I don't know how I could have got that impression, seeing her in dripping shorts, which clung to long, slender legs, and a wet shirt, but I did. She was exactly what I might have expected of George Bronson's wife; yet in another and subtle way, which I felt rather than defined, she wasn't at all what I might have expected.

She had a rather hoarse voice which yet was attractive, and

74

as she saw me hunting through the closets and opening drawers she laughed and took over. "Never mind what you give me. Anything will do. How about this?"

She slid out of her clothes and into mine almost before I could bring her a towel, said hoarsely that if you dried in the saddle you never took cold and fastened up my skirt. She yanked at the shirt, grinned, again rather like a cat, said that was the way clothes ought to be made, just a little too tight, and then eyed me rather like a mischievous child. "It would shock Alice if I said anything like that. What a fake that woman is!"

I had thought a great many things of Alice but I hadn't thought that. Nadine chuckled, hoarsely too, and took my comb. "Mind if I use this? I've got to do something with my hair. The rain caught me out at the very end of the island, in all that muddy marsh, and I thought I'd never find my way back to human habitation. Finally I saw your light."

She was shouting as John and I had shouted. She whirled my comb through her hair, and with an expertise which held me spellbound, smoothed, brushed, twisted and suddenly had a smooth and very elegant cap of reddish hair. Even in my faded brown skirt and a shirt which had seen many launderings, she was chic, sleek and smart. She picked up her discarded clothing, went off to the bathroom and efficiently and neatly hung everything up on the shower rail. "Sorry," she said over her shoulder. "I'm afraid they'll have to stay here for a little. Mind if I borrow your clothes until mine dry? I brought only enough for the weekend. I meant what I said, you know, about Alice."

She gave a smoothing kind of tug to my skirt and smiled at me. "I feel better. Can you put up with me until the rain stops? That is, if it does stop on this devil's island. What a place! I didn't want to come, you know. George coaxed me into it. Then that other pestiferous woman managed to get herself dead."

She was going down the stairs, moving like a streak. I took a leaf out of John's book and said, "Huh—"

She reached the last step, took one glance around the room and chose John's rocking chair. "I mean Mildred, of course.

My private opinion is that somebody hit her over the head."

I think I gulped. She sat down in the chair and tipped experimentally backward. "I've always liked a rocking chair. So you think somebody hit her over the head, too."

"No!"

"Now, now," she said with a kind of cool yet queerly friendly derision in her green eyes. "I'm Nadine. Don't try to tell me stories. But it doesn't matter. Just so long as nobody else thinks she was murdered. Except, of course, George wants to get out. I can't say I like staying around here either."

"He said—"

She shot me a glance. "Ah, you've seen him."

"Yes, he came to see Tom."

She interrupted again. "Tom Esseven, yes. Your husband. He went with Boyd. Boyd certainly needs somebody to hold his hand. No, I agree with George. I'm going to leave that haunted house if I have to swim for it."

The conversation was becoming obscured again, as it had with John. Part of the confusion was due to the steady drum of the rain, but part was due to what I began to recognize as the swift agility of Nadine's mind, which shot here and there like a hummingbird and with as sharp and needlelike a beak. She said, "I mean Mildred's house. That is, it's not a real house. It's a silly make-believe. A completely new and sparkling copy of an old Maine coast house. There are more cherry-wood chests and moth-eaten samplers and flatiron doorstops than you can count." She rocked and brooded rather crossly. "All of it apple-pie neat and shining. Makes me want to take one of the flatiron doorstops and throw it through one of those fake bull's-eye windows. Oh, well, that's childish. Boyd shouldn't have killed her, really. That's a childish thing to do too. Murder never settles anything."

"It wasn't—Boyd didn't—"

"Or Tom," said Nadine and didn't even bother to look at me but rocked and thought.

I took a cigarette and then was afraid to light it because my hands might be unsteady, and I had a notion that Nadine's sparkling green eyes never missed anything. She was looking very thoughtful; she said, "Tom's got more character than

Boyd. Still, I suppose Boyd or anybody could conceivably work himself up to a rage and hit somebody on the head too hard without considering the consequences. Yet Tom certainly didn't want Mildred to make Boyd sell the business. Yes, I'd pick Tom as first murderer." She looked up at me and her eyes widened. "For heaven's sake, child. Don't look like that. They said it was an accident. Call it accident. I'm one for letting sleeping dogs lie—or sleeping murderers."

"Tom didn't kill her. It really was"—I swallowed but got it out—"an accident."

She grinned, exactly like a cat again, hunting out a nice mouse. "Okay, all right, fine. Accident. How'd you manage this elopement business? Never mind. That's none of my business either. But Alice! I wouldn't have missed that for anything."

"I'm—" I think I intended to say lamely that I was sorry about Alice.

Nadine didn't permit it. Her grin became broader and franker. "She was fit to be tied," she said with a hoarse chuckle. "Little Miss Muffet robbed of her husband. Little Lady Macbeth, if you ask me. When I told you to avoid Alice on a dark night I meant it. The rain's stopped."

It had. With the disconcerting suddenness of all our summer storms, it had stopped as if it had never been. All at once everything seemed very still. Somewhere a bird gave a wary twitter.

Nadine stopped rocking to listen and then looked at me cautiously. "Is this comparative calm going to last?"

"I think so."

"I doubt it." She rose and bit her lower lip. "George wants to leave and so do I, and if I don't trail him down this minute, Alice will be making a play for him." She flicked one green glance at me and said as if it explained something, "Money. George is very rich."

"But Alice is—that is, was—engaged to Tom."

"You married him, dearie. Good for you. Tom is very attractive. But really, you should have seen Alice yesterday. First she couldn't understand where Tom had gone, and then she began to ask about you and came down here to the cottage and came flying back and said you were gone, too. She had her jaw set—did you ever happen to notice that sometimes she looks exactly like Mildred? I mean, something way back in her eyes? Birds of a feather, if you ask me, but Alice is smarter. She can put on this sweet and feminine act. She guessed you and Tom had gone off to get married—I'm sure of that. She tackled John Cobwell and got no change from him. Then she tackled the human turtle."

"Turtle—"

"What's his name? Writes nonsense about duels and tournaments—"

"Greenleaf Whittier Trace."

"That's it. He just pulled in his chin and ran. And then Alice tackled the Sahib. I think he had his heart attack as much to escape her as to get out of all the unpleasantness that was going on here, sheriff, everything." She broke off. "Sahib. That's a silly kind of nickname. Why?"

"I don't know. He's always been called the Sahib."

"So George said." She seemed to brood over that too, and sighed. "Oh, well, it takes all kinds. He's a bit of a fake, too, your Sahib—"

"He's the best friend I ever had in my life—"

"Now, now, I've heard all about that. He's all right. But he likes to put on a show. I doubt if he had a real heart attack."

"He does have a bad heart. It's why he retired."

"I don't suppose that they'll sell the business to George now."

"I don't know. I didn't even know that Mr. Bronson had made an offer for it until—" Until I had heard Mildred shouting at Tom the night she was murdered. I said, "Until recently."

Nadine sighed again. "George has got about as much notion of how to run a publishing company as I have about how to develop an oil well. That's how George got all his money." She went to the door and opened it. Beyond her everything dripped and was very green but still. She said casually over her shoulder, "Mildred talked George into trying to buy the Esseven company, you know."

"*Mildred* did!"

78

"Oh, yes. She met him somewhere. Latched on to him. All at once George began to see himself as a big culture tycoon. Mildred was a powerful woman, don't think she wasn't."

"Yes, I know."

"But Alice is smarter. Remember that." She waited a second, and I didn't say anything. She laughed. "That's right, friend. Keep a tight mouth. Well, in any event, George can forget about this particular ambition. He'll do something else, though. He was talking about backing some plays only this morning. If Alice thinks she can get her hooks into him now that you got Tom away from her, I'll stop that. I've got the best of far more skillful women than Alice, believe me. I was telling you what happened yesterday when the telegram came from Tom, saying you and he were married. She hung on to George finally, yesterday, and began to work on his sympathies. George's got a heart like jelly—"

That had not been my impression. However, Nadine must know best. She went on, "He's also got a free and roving eye. Goodbye."

It surprised me a little to discover that George Bronson had thought it expedient to tell so smooth a lie, saying that his wife Nadine was devoted to Mildred; clearly she was not. But it did not surprise me to learn that Mildred had originated the idea of selling the business and selling it to George Bronson, who, as his wife said, had money. I might have guessed that if I had given any thought to it. But I did not for a moment think that Bronson could possibly have been attracted to Mildred.

Still, Mildred must have attracted Boyd once, although it had always seemed to me that Mildred, even then, had simply overpowered him. Their marriage had occurred during my schooldays; I was summoned home from school for the wedding and sat in the pew beside the Sahib, who looked very grand with a boutonniere. My first glimpse of Mildred, in fact, was when she put back her white veil and grasped Boyd's arm with a firm hand as they marched away from the altar. By the time I had come to the island for the summer, Mildred was established as the lady of the house. We didn't like each other —from the first I had the feeling that she looked upon me as an interloper—but we were polite.

79

I wouldn't let myself think of Mildred's murder, not there and then, alone in the cottage with a little drip of rain from twigs and leaves surrounding the cottage, everywhere a tiny, almost ghostlike patter.

It occurred to me to telephone Mrs. Mapping and ask whether or not she had left a hammer in my bedroom, but the thought of the switchboard at Piney Point deterred me. I also thought of Henrietta, Mrs. Mapping's daughter, who was as bright-eyed and curious as a little hen and was dramatic. She picked up crumbs of anything at all that happened on the island, and instinctively her theatrical sense had its way by building these crumbs into probably horrendous stories to tell her friends at Piney Point. Henrietta must be having the time of her life now.

The steady tiny drip outside began to bother me; the birds twittered a little now and then, but not happily somehow, rather in a warning way as they do before a storm.

But Nadine was wrong about Alice; Alice might be another and smarter Mildred, but she couldn't be a fake. She had charm, and until the previous night when I had caught that odd glimpse of physical strength and toughness about her, she had seemed to me the very epitome of rather frail and appealing feminine beauty. I knew that in fact she was a gifted woman, and perhaps this too had appealed to Tom. She had whizzed through the most expensive schools; she had studied painting and music in Paris and in Rome, She had enough money, apparently; she dressed well and expensively. Her father lived in Rome and she visited him and spoke Italian as well as she spoke French. She had poise and grace. She was a most formidable opponent. The plain fact was that if I hadn't wanted Tom myself I'd have thought Alice the perfect wife for him. Clearly he had thought so too. Tom was not naïve; he hadn't been dazzled by Alice; he'd fallen in love with her barely a few weeks after they had met.

I went to the big house.

It was very wet along the path. The strip of beach was wet, too, and the sand clung to my sneakers. The runabout again lay tied out at the end of the pier. The sky was still heavy and dark but very quiet, rather as if it didn't know exactly what it was going to do, but whatever it was, it wouldn't be very pleasant. The sound had a slow, sullen roll to it, and the runabout rocked. There were no sails around Piney Point and only one motorboat close to the shore. I started up the long flights of steps to the big house.

Shallow patches of rain water made the steps a little slippery and treacherous. Here, too, everywhere there was a steady drip and murmur which followed me up the steps almost as if something invisible were pursuing me. I went on, winding around, thinking of how, when I was young, I had counted the steps in groups; I had known just how many there were between landings. I counted them and found that I still knew, and reached the last flight of five steps up to the wide porch of the big house.

Alice, Leaf Trace, George Bronson and Nadine sat there. The old chairs were uncomfortably stiff and heavy, owing as much perhaps to the many coats of white paint that had been given them over the years as to their original weight. I caught my breath, and George Bronson's free and roving eyes fixed themselves upon my legs, Alice's lovely face turned to pink and white stone, and Nadine turned away from them toward me and gave me a prodigious wink which took me into a conspiracy of intervention between Alice and George Bronson. "Come and sit," Nadine said.

Leaf was huddled in his long black leather coat. He cast a lackluster eye at me and popped a pill into his mouth, as if murder might be contagious and he wished to ward off an attack of it. I said that I wanted to see the Sahib and went into the house.

The hall was exactly as it had been the night I had come into it and seen Alice's pink sweater and the hammer and newspaper on the bench. A raincoat lay there now. The clock at the end of the hall reminded me that it was well past lunchtime, so I went into the dining room—a room which to most people would seem a chamber of horrors, with its oak wainscoting and the painting of a watermelon, cut open and surrounded by ghastly pink peaches, which hung above a fancifully carved oak mantel. There was a chandelier above the table which was an inverted bowl of segments of green and purple glass, guaranteed to shed a deathly light upon any face below it. I could understand why strangers might be revolted by the room (for that matter the whole house left much to be desired in the way of aesthetics), but to me it was merely a part of my life.

I went on into the pantry. As always, Mrs. Mapping had left enough food for both houses, the Sahib's and Boyd's, cooked and ready for us. The others had apparently already lunched; there were dishes and glasses, shoved hit-or-miss around the pantry, which Mrs. Mapping would not like. We had been under Mrs. Mapping's thumb—a benevolent thumb, for the most part—for so long that I had started automatically to straighten up the pantry when Leaf came in. "How can you eat at such a time?" he said.

"I'm not eating yet."

"All this food!" He waved one hand at it in horror.

"I'm hungry. Didn't you eat?"

"Oh, I managed to choke down something. One must keep up one's strength. I think I'll just have some of that pie, as a matter of fact." He took up a knife and cut off a big slab of pie.

"I think you'll bear up, Leaf, really I do," I said.

He turned on me in indignation and said, with pie in his mouth, which rather detracted from the dignified outrage of his manner, "Do you realize that the sheriff told me I had to stay here! He didn't even say how long! I know nothing of this dreadful accident. Why—why—" He gulped down the pie and his Adam's apple moved above his black leather coat. "Why, it's as if Mildred had been murdered. Actually!"

"They said it was an accident."

"That's right! That's what they said, but why did the sheriff ask me exactly where I was that night, tell me that? Why did he give me such a strange look when I said I'd been sitting on a rock on the south shore for over an hour? I really was, you know. I explained it to him. I was thinking about my new book—not the one you have but the next one. An artist falls into these moods. I wouldn't have seen Mildred if she walked straight up to me." He gave me a horrified glance. "Not that she did, you understand. I left the house as soon as she began

82

to yell at—I mean discuss the matter of selling the business with Tom. It was a family affair, so I left."

"Of course." I wished that he would leave now.

He eyed me vacantly yet accusingly. "Where was Tom that night, when I stopped in at the cottage?"

"Wh—what?"

"I understood that you and Tom were planning your elopement, just then. Where was he?"

Another lie. "In the kitchen. He didn't want to talk to you just then."

Leaf blinked but accepted it. "Oh." He took the sharp and shining knife again to cut some more pie. He suddenly perceived its sharpness and put it down with a clatter and a shudder. "I might have cut myself!" He swallowed the rest of his pie at a gulp and scurried out of the pantry.

No, I decided, Leaf could never have approached Mildred and wrested the hammer from her, not Leaf.

As usual, the food Mrs. Mapping and Henrietta prepared for Sunday actually was enough to last over Monday, which may or may not have been canny planning on their part. In any event, I had cold chicken and ham and salad and what apple pie Leaf had left, and felt better. Everything seemed about to return itself to a normal Sunday noon.

Except that the normal Sunday noon custom was luncheon, with all of us gathered around the big table in the dining room; this habit was due in part to the Sahib's patriarchal notion of having his family around him—unless we annoyed him and he stalked haughtily away—but most of it was due to Mrs. Mapping's firm stand about cooking. She hadn't liked Mildred and she wouldn't cook at Boyd's house, which she disliked. If Mildred and Boyd elected to have lunch with the Sahib, then they were in the position of guests and Mrs. Mapping did not object.

It was close to four o'clock when I went to see the Sahib. The hall door was open as usual, and through the screen the sky looked more threatening, as if it had about made up its mind. The wide hall upstairs had faded oriental rugs placed at spots almost sure to trip anybody who wasn't accustomed to them. I stopped at the open door of the Sahib's great corner room. He had heard me coming and I guessed had not been sure who it was, for he was giving such an impersonation of extreme illness that I stopped for a second, appalled.

He was lying back on the pillows, his eyes closed, an indescribable expression of noble and courageous sickness on his face. But I noted that his brilliant yellow scarf was becomingly arranged, that he wore a Chinese silk robe of some kind, glittering with gold threads, and that his fringe of white curls was neatly brushed. He opened one eye cautiously, then sat up and in a perfectly healthy and natural voice, said, "Oh, it's you. I wasn't sure."

"You scared me."

"I do it rather well, don't I," he said complacently. "Give me a cigarette. There's a box over on that table. If anybody objects, I'll say it was you smoking. Have one yourself."

"You really are an old—" Nadine's word fake came into my mind, but that wasn't right either. He supplied the word: "Actor? Or fraud? Never mind, shut that door."

I obeyed, and brought him the cigarettes he was not supposed to have, lighted one for him and one for myself and pushed an ashtray near him. "Well," he said again complacently, "everything is going very well. Just as I told you. Accident."

"The sheriff doesn't think so."

He considered this and replied with unruffled smugness. "No. He's snooping around. So you see I was right in getting you married to Tom."

"Actually, I think that was what made him suspicious. He came to exactly the right conclusion—"

He interrupted me. "Not at all. He'd have been suspicious no matter what we did or didn't do. He's a very intelligent man."

"He knows us too well."

The Sahib looked thoughtful. "Maybe he knows me too well, knows what I might do and why I might do it. I don't like to admit it, but sometimes he beats me at chess."

"He beats you quite often, as I remember it," I said crossly. "He said that my marriage to Tom would make it possible for

84

me to refuse to testify against him if I had any evidence and if Mildred was murdered."

"But he said *if*," the Sahib said triumphantly. "He's got a good mind, fast, logical, but there's nothing he can do and he knows it. You see how right I was in getting you and Tom married."

"You railroaded us into that. You terrified me. Tom didn't want to."

"Oh, don't fuss," the Sahib said and put his hand over his heart and gave me a wicked glance. "I'll have a real heart attack if you do."

"You're quite capable of it, just to get your own way." This was true, but since I loved the Sahib the words came out like a compliment.

"My own way is the right way. You won't admit it but it is."

"It was all wrong." This did not come out like a compliment; it was bitterly true. "Tom is in love with Alice. How soon can I get out of this marriage?"

He gave me a piercing, swift look. "Don't talk like that, Sissy. You're married to Tom. You can't do anything about getting out of it now. Do I have to tell you again that this is your chance! Make the most of it."

There was no use in pretending either to the Sahib or to myself that something way back in my mind had not suggested such a course. But the plain fact was that while it was possible to imagine hurling myself into Tom's surprised arms, it was also far too easy to imagine what a fool I'd make of myself and Tom.

The Sahib's eyes narrowed. "If this marriage continues to be the kind of thing which I suspect it is now, then I have brought up two idiot children, you and Tom," he said coldly.

"You don't know a thing about it," I began angrily when someone knocked lightly on the door and opened it. Alice came in. She looked past me, smiled at the Sahib and came to stand between us, looking down at him. "Tom just phoned," she said. "He wanted me to tell you that their plane was delayed by the storm. They'll be late getting home tonight."

chapter 8

"Thank you, my dear," the Sahib said. "Did he say how late?"

"I don't think he knew. He said there is a squall line."

Alice's pink linen dress was marvelously unwrinkled that humid day. The dress was sleeveless, showing her white yet unexpectedly muscular arms. I wondered vaguely whether she ever wore any color but pink, and decided that if not, snow and slushy winter weather must pose certain problems. But now the pink and white and gold looked lovely, enhanced by Tom's diamond on her hand.

She moved to a chair and glanced at me. "The Sahib likes somebody to read to him." She reached for a volume of Gibbon which lay on the bedside table.

It was as if she were already a part of the family and I was a stranger; I knew that the Sahib liked to be read to, and I had planned to read to him once we had finished our talk. The Sahib said, "Thank you, my dear. I'll see you later, Sissy."

It was a dismissal, but knowing the Sahib it wouldn't have bothered me if Alice had not been there to witness it. I knew that the Sahib merely sensed a storm coming on my part and wished to avoid it, but Alice smiled smugly as a kitten, tossed back that long lock which kept falling over her face and opened the book.

So I left. I drifted through the living room, where again I could almost see Mildred standing before the piano, her hand planted on it, her sturdy legs planted solidly, too, as she told Tom what he must do and Tom had lost his temper and said, "Some day I'm going to kill you."

There had been the hint of a clash when Mildred had demanded Alice's support in the question of selling the business and Alice had refused it.

Speculation can get the bit in its teeth and careen wildly along almost any path; the path it then chose suggested a quarrel, swift and terrible, between Alice and Mildred, and a hammer in Alice's beautiful strong hands.

I had absently picked up a small china ornament, a little shepherdess with an insipid smile. I put it down again hurriedly, dismayed at the course of my fancy. My wedding ring gleamed. But Alice had the diamond ring.

The mirror over the mantel cast back my reflection weirdly, so my face looked white against the gloom of the room. I avoided a French settee, gilt and brocade, entirely out of place in that house, and an umbrella stand made from an elephant's foot which would have been out of place in any house, and went back to the hell room.

Here, too, nothing had changed except that a dead moth lay below the table lamp. There was Tom's yellow tablet on the table, exactly as I had left it. I flicked the moth gently into the wastebasket. It had been a lovely thing, all mauve and white; now it was shriveled and sad.

The fact was that I had married a man who didn't want to marry me, and this absurd kind of marriage could go on for months—even for years, I thought, feeling thoroughly glum. It was very likely that for the rest of my life Tom would call me Sister and think of me as a sister. I wished I'd had the plain common sense to stay away from Scatawan Island that summer.

There was only one decent thing to do about Alice, and that was to tell her the whole story. I had known it in my heart from the beginning; I hadn't wanted to acknowledge it but I could duck the issue no longer. I didn't know just how I was going to develop such nobility in my own nature, but there was no denying the fact that in fairness to Tom and to Alice it had to be done. It was true that I couldn't bring myself to care much about Alice's feelings; I couldn't become that noble all at once. But I did care about Tom.

Gradually it grew darker, and when the clock in the hall struck six I started back to the cottage.

There was a light in the hall. Alice was nowhere to be seen and I couldn't hear the sound of her light, musical voice reading to the Sahib. It occurred to me that I might go up to his room and offer to bring him supper, but I decided that Alice could continue her daughterly role and take it to him.

On the porch the chairs and settees loomed up ghostily in their many layers of white paint. There were small whitecaps out toward the east end of the island and only a stretch of sullen-looking water between the island and Piney Point. As I stood on the porch the light at Crab Island came on and shot its rays out into the murky sky. There was no one on the porch now and it was chilly. I started down the flights of steps. The steps were still wet, but the puddles of rain had disappeared. At the first landing I paused and again looked out toward Piney Point. But no boat was heading for the island, and of course there would not have been time for Tom and Boyd to arrive at the airport, let alone drive to Piney Point and get Wally Rutherford or one of the other men who had boats for hire to bring them to the island. I wished that I had thought to ask Alice where Tom had been when he telephoned. I went on down.

I had taken three or four steps of the longest group, the forty steps, when my foot slithered and slipped. I managed to clutch the railing as the step seemed to quiver and slide away from me. Somehow I held on to the railing and found myself half squirmed under it, sprawling anyhow on rocks and wet pine needles, with a splinter in my palm and my ankle turned under me. The strangely slippery step seemed to bounce down half the flight and came to rest upside down.

It was not a step at all. It was a piece of wood, rectangular, with wheels in the air, still rotating. It was a child's skateboard.

I ducked under the railing again and onto a real step, sucked my palm and stared at the skateboard. If I had stumbled over one of my old roller skates I wouldn't have been surprised. I had never used roller skates on the island—there was no suitable place for roller-skating—but any of our toys, baseball bats or sleds or roller skates might easily have been transferred from the city house to the island at some time merely for that useless kind of storage which happens when children grow up and nobody quite knows what to do with the bits and pieces left over from childhood.

But this was a skateboard, a recent fad for the young fry, and there were no young fry on the island. It didn't look new; rather, it had received a certain amount of battering. It was not a toy to induce confidence in anybody, for as far as I knew there was no way at all of governing its course and it required the balance and poise of a young Mercury to manipulate.

If I hadn't caught the railing in time I would have shot down the entire flight of steps and perhaps been killed. It was a perfect instrument of murder, lying on the steps like that, so much resembling a step if an unwary person didn't happen to look closely, as I had not.

John had warned me that I was a witness, but I had only seen Tom trying to save Mildred, not trying to kill her. Boyd might have believed that I had seen more. But Boyd was not on the island and so couldn't have placed the skateboard in that innocent-appearing yet potentially deadly position. Boyd and Tom were together. Boyd and Tom had always been together; they had always supported each other. But Tom wouldn't have tried to kill me with that absurd, that preposterous—that deadly instrument of murder!

It astonished me in an odd, almost objective way, as if I were looking at myself from the outside, that I had even thought of Tom as a possible source of danger. I felt as if something cold had knocked at my heart.

I got up and went cautiously down the steps. I picked up the skateboard and examined it closely, but it was only a skateboard, battered and worn, which looked as if some child had lost it. But certainly somebody had brought it to the island, and that argued a purpose.

The skateboard had been left—so innocently, as if by accident—near the top of the steps which I would take to return to the cottage. Alice and the two Bronsons would have taken the other direction, the close and easy path that went around behind the big house and sloped downward to Boyd's new house on the south shore.

It was dark among the close-growing pines, and I could hear a murmur of the waves below. I didn't even think of going back up those steps to the big house. I went on down, but very carefully, thinking that there might be other traps along the way. I crossed the beach and hurried along the path. Everything in the cottage was exactly as I had left it.

I looked around the living room and into the kitchen for other traps. I didn't know what I was looking for, except that if such a thing existed, I should be able to see it or even sense it. There was nothing. I hid the skateboard in the woodbox, stuffing it down below the kindling; I did not know just why I did that, either.

The dank odors of old fires came from the fireplace, as always during wet weather. I opened the casement windows, above the crimson-cushioned window seat, which I had closed when the rain came. The cool moist air was refreshing. By then it was very black outside and a few moths arrived instantly, fluttering against the indoor screens.

My palm smarted. I had grazed my knee and that smarted too. I examined the splinter and all at once a monstrous and hateful logic took over. Logic has a ruthless way of its own; once started, there is nothing to be done to stop it.

There had been the hammer on my dressing table; later it was gone, but it was a reminder of Mildred's death which logic could—and did just then—choose as an argument. There had been the skateboard, another logical argument.

Tom was the only person to whom I was in fact a potential danger. Tom could have met Mildred by chance at the boathouse, and Mildred could have resumed their quarrel. Logic suggested a moment of ungovernable, irrational impulse on Tom's part which he could not control. So the hammer smashed down upon Mildred's head. And then immediately Tom could have come to his senses, and so he would have tried to pull her out of the water. Or perhaps he had not come to his senses, had only known that he must make sure that she was dead. Logic even went so far as to suggest that Tom was not

90

trying to rescue her when I came on the scene; instead he was holding her under the water to make sure that she died.

He could not have expected me to arrive when I did and see what I had seen. It was perfectly possible that he had not chanced to pick up the hammer, that in fact he was still holding it in his hand.

Logic went on. The Sahib's plan for our marriage offered a way to keep me quiet about what I had seen. Tom had been reluctant, but that could have been a calculated reluctance and in the end he had yielded. His seeming candor could have been the most adroit deception. He would have known that I would believe whatever he said; that added another argument to logic.

Tom had telephoned and talked to Alice that evening, only an hour or so before, and said that he and Boyd had been delayed by the storm. Logic said that in fact one or both of them could have quietly returned to the island and placed the skateboard in its murderous position. This, however, did not seem as powerful an argument as the others; besides, it could easily be proved just when Tom and Boyd arrived at the airport and at Piney Point. But, of course, not at this minute, not right now.

Mildred had been determined to sell the company; Tom had opposed her, and he had known that she would go over Boyd like a steam roller. The Sahib, John, the sheriff—all three suspected Tom or Boyd. Even Nadine had chosen Tom as the more likely murderer of the two of them.

Willy, nilly, said remorseless logic, Tom was the only person I threatened.

So logic was all wrong! No logic, no argument, not even my own eyes could make me believe that Tom had murdered Mildred.

My whole body had seemed numb and chill; now the warmth and living pulses seemed to return. It was as if I had been under an evil spell and was now released. And then in the rush of thankfulness for my escape I saw an argument which stood against logic; the hammer had been placed on my dressing table sometime while Tom and I were away from the island; Tom had had no opportunity to leave a hammer there.

And in fact the hammer might not have been a mute threat at all; a reasonable explanation for anything is always likeliest to be the true explanation. Still, a hammer cannot move of its own volition, so the reasonable explanation was not so reasonable.

The skateboard did not have any reasonable explanation at all.

I sucked at the splinter in my hand as my thoughts went galloping on. A stumble over the skateboard, a fall down the long flight of steps would not necessarily be fatal; indeed, it was far more likely merely to turn an ankle or even break a wrist. It might frighten somebody. It certainly had frightened somebody: me.

But if I had fallen, if by any remote chance the fall had injured me, if it had killed me, certainly the sheriff would not accept the possibility of two fatal accidents on the island occurring so close together; he'd be sure then that there was indeed something fishy. However, it was not exactly comforting to reflect that such a contingency would arise only if I had been very neatly murdered.

There was the scuffle of a foot on the step. I thought Tom was returning and ran to the door, but it was John.

He had his pipe in his hand. "I've been sitting down there at the pier watching for Tom and Boyd," he said. "Time they're getting home. But the radio says there are thunderstorms all around. They may not be able to get home until late." He went to the rocking chair. "I think Tom meant to talk to you when he phoned a while ago. Alice happened to be in the hall near the phone."

"It doesn't matter."

"I thought I'd tell you." He dug into a pocket for his pipe. "The sheriff saw the padlock on the boathouse door. I mean the hasp, where it was pulled out. Mildred must have started to pry it out—I got it fully out later when I got down the dinghy and—"

"Yes, I know. I heard you tell the Sahib that night."

"Well, if the sheriff asks you about the padlock and who pried it out, tell him I did when we found Mildred. I wanted to get a blanket out of the Ark to cover her. I thought there might be a blanket left in a locker, but there wasn't. That's what I told him."

"All right." Another lie. I'd have to start making notes on all the lies; otherwise I'd trap myself in them. And in the same instant another lie, a very urgent one, surged up in my mind. I didn't want to prove that Boyd had killed Mildred—or at least had been on the island and had the opportunity to kill her—but I did have to give myself and logic a strong argument which would tend to prove that Tom had not killed her. So the lie came straight out of my lips as if I'd planned it a long time. "John, I saw you in the runabout the night Mildred was killed."

I had not allowed for John's slight deafness. He said, "Of course you saw me that night! I was here—"

I said loudly, "In the runabout. You were in the runabout. I saw you."

He heard that and shook his head. "You said that it was so dark and foggy that you couldn't see anybody in the runabout."

"I know. I was confused. I hadn't had time to think about it. But now . . . It *was* Boyd with you, wasn't it?"

John gave me a long, discerning look. "You are trying to prove to yourself that Tom didn't kill Mildred, and that Boyd was here on the island and had the opportunity. My dear, even if I had seen Boyd—as I didn't—I would never tell anybody, and I advise you to keep quiet." He rose. "Now, you've been doing very well so far. If you keep it up, we may get everybody out of this without any more questions asked. I think, myself, that the sheriff's gone about as far as he can go without making some kind of open statement to the effect that he thinks it was murder. He's got no proof of that and he's not the kind of man to put himself out on a limb without any way to crawl back . . . Goodnight, Sister."

When John had gone the cottage seemed lonely and quiet. I could hear only the faint whisper of waves down at the shoreline and now and then a sleepy rustle of a bird in some thicket. I listened for the sound of a boat bringing Tom back to the island. The cottage, though, seemed to take on a kind of waiting

93

life of its own. There was nobody there at all. I'd have heard the faintest shuffle of a foot, the faintest rustle of clothes; I'd even have heard anybody breathing, I was sure of that.

My palm and knee smarted, so I went up the little stairway intending to apply tweezers and antiseptics. I had already turned on lights; the bathroom was shining and empty of human presence, as I had known it would be. My bedroom was lighted and nobody was there; I had known that too. So I felt like a fool when I went to the closet and opened it, although it was so shallow, built in under the eaves, that a cat could scarcely have hidden there. Turning from it I happened to see myself in the mirror over the dressing table; I looked white and tousled as a witch on a broomstick on a windy night. I went to the dressing table and without looking reached for my brush and picked up a hammer.

I actually had it in my hand before its weight and a sense of unfamiliarity struck me and I looked down and dropped it. I dropped it so hard that it clattered on the top of the dressing table, knocking over my bottle of expensive perfume, which fell to the floor. The hammer fell too with a horrible thud. The fragrance of lilacs rose from the broken perfume bottle, so sweet and strong that I felt dizzy.

I whirled around and started for the stairs. I would telephone to the big house. I'd tell John or somebody to come and get me.

At the top of the stairs I saw something which I had not seen before. It lay on the polished floor of the tiny hall. It was a lump of wet sand; it looked as if it had fallen from somebody's shoe.

Only Nadine, to my knowledge, had been upstairs since the rain began. The lump of sand was too wet to have fallen from one of her sneakers; that would have dried a little during the interval. This tiny chunk of sand had fallen there recently, within an hour, perhaps within moments. I couldn't have said how long it had been there, but I knew that it wasn't long.

So somebody had come into the cottage and brought the hammer back.

From where I stood, I could see down into the living room.

Then I saw the door open, very slowly and very quietly, and I couldn't move.

Alice came in. She cast a look around, so queerly sly and yet so intent that without meaning to I slid back so that she couldn't see me at the top of the stairs.

I couldn't see her. But I could hear her. There was a long pause, as if she were testing the silence in the cottage. Then she moved away from the door; I could barely hear the motion. There were no places to hide anything in the room, or indeed in the whole cottage—except of course the woodbox. All at once I heard the dull little bang of its top. So Alice had opened it, very quietly, and now had closed it again.

I crouched down until I could see below the railing. She was standing at the table, the skateboard in her hands. Tom's big diamond caught the light and winked and glittered at me.

Perhaps I made some move. I saw her stiffen, as if she heard something; then she lifted her head and said, "Come down here. I know you're there. I can smell your perfume."

..........chapter 9..........

I rose, and in the same second I must have cast off the last remnants of the conventional and well-behaved young lady I had thought myself only a short time before. I marched down the stairs and said, "What are you doing here?"

Her blue eyes widened a little, as if surprised, but then hardened. "Why did you hide this?" She held out the skateboard.

"Why did you creep into my cottage and hunt for it?"

"*Your* cottage—"

"Certainly. I'm Tom's wife, remember?"

She stared at me for a moment. I felt a little drunk with power, I suppose, and said lightly, "With all my worldly goods I thee endow. It's part of the marriage ceremony."

She put the skateboard down on the table, very slowly. Then as slowly she sat down and looked at me. "You're very sure of yourself, aren't you?"

Still half intoxicated with my own daring I said lightly, "Why not?"

She thought that over. "I can tell you several reasons why not. I saw you stumble on that skateboard."

The intoxication of defying Alice had really gone to my head. I said, "Really. Did you put it there on the step?"

She thought again. "No," she said at last. "I didn't. Who did?"

"I don't know."

"Then why did you hide it?"

"Why did you creep in here to look for it?"

She bit her lip and lowered her stony blue gaze.

This kind of exchange was going to get neither of us anywhere. I said, "Alice, I really don't know who left the skateboard on the steps. What do you know about it?"

"I came out on the porch as you went down the steps. I saw you stumble. Then further down the steps I saw you pick up something and look at it, and"—she took a breath and lifted her bright blue gaze—"so I came to see what it was."

"Why didn't you just ask me to tell you about it?"

She linked her white hands and frowned down at them. Tom's diamond winked and glittered. "Sister, there is something happening on this island that I don't understand."

My guard flashed up as if alarms had rung. "What do you mean?"

"You know perfectly well what I mean. It's been like this since Mildred's death. Was Mildred murdered?"

It caught me unexpectedly. "Murdered! What a thing to say!"

"Oh, I'm no fool. The sheriff hanging around asking me all those questions: Where were you? How did it happen that you didn't know that Mildred had not come home that night?" She paused, turned the diamond ring on her finger and said flatly, "I went home alone after that quarrel Mildred had with Tom. I didn't see Mildred again. I didn't know that Mildred hadn't come back until the next morning. And she—we were friends."

I said, "Were you friends, Alice?"

"Certainly!"

"Alice, that night when Mildred died—I mean when she and you and Tom were talking—she wanted you to support her decision to sell the business. She said that perhaps you wouldn't be a very good wife to Tom. What did she mean?"

Alice sprang up, her face stony white. "What do *you* mean? Are you accusing me of murder? Are you trying to say that Mildred knew something of me that I—why, that I would murder to keep quiet? What about yourself? Why did Tom take you off across the country to marry you? Was it only because you made him feel that he owed you marriage? Or was it something else? Do you know anything about Mildred's—" She caught herself before she said murder. I had put out my hand, almost as if I must defend myself physically, and she saw the gleam of my wedding ring and cried, "You're wearing a wedding ring. It should be my wedding ring and you know it. You stole Tom from me. You've got to give him back. You've got to end this silly marriage. Tom doesn't want you."

The trouble with that was that it was the truth.

I surged up out of the rocking chair, which tipped back and struck my legs smartly. "You're wearing Tom's diamond. Give it to me."

Alice opened her mouth; actually, it hung open for a second, as if she were struck dumb. "Why, you—" she said then. "Why, you're positively dangerous. You've changed!"

"I'll not leave Tom. Nobody can make me. And he does want me for his wife. He married me, didn't he?"

I stopped because the door was flung open behind me and Tom came in, his raincoat over his arm. Boyd followed him. Both of them looked disheveled and tired, and Boyd was grinning. So I knew that they had heard me.

Tom said, "Hello. Sorry we're so late."

Boyd reached for the rocking chair and sank wearily into it. His handsome face was flushed and his eyes glassy and I knew that he'd been drinking.

Alice faced Tom, her lovely head up; she wasn't breathing fire but she was close to it. "Tom, you heard us. You heard what Sister said."

Tom put down his raincoat carefully. Then he turned to Alice. He didn't look at me. "Yes," he said, "you were both—"

"Screaming," Boyd said and giggled.

"Shut up, Boyd." Tom went to Alice and put out his hand; she put her own hand in it, and he said seriously, "I'm sorry, Alice. I ought to have explained. I ought to have taken the bull by the horns."

It was too apt an expression, for Alice really did look as if she might snort and paw. Tom said, "It simply happened the way it happened, Alice. Our marriage, I mean. My marriage to Sister—"

"Mustn't say sister," Boyd mumbled behind me. "Indecent.

98

Call her—what in hell is your name, Sister? Something stuffy, can't remember—"

"Will you shut up, Boyd," Tom said.

Alice drew closer to Tom. She put her other hand on his shoulder. "But you love me, Tom. How could you change like this? Tom, I don't believe you've changed. I believe there's some—some other reason for this elopement. You're still in love with me."

Boyd leaned forward; he even took my wrist and moved me a little to one side so that he could observe Alice and Tom. He said, smiling, "Just like a show. Go on, make up your mind, Tom. Can't have two wives, you know. Which is it, Alice or Sister? I remember—Cornelia! That's her name, Cornelia—your wife, Cornelia."

"Boyd," Tom said, "if you don't shut up I'll throw you out. I mean it."

Alice still kept her hand on Tom's shoulder. Her lovely face was turned up appealingly to him. She said, very gently, "Why, she even wants the ring you gave me. This beautiful diamond you gave me when we promised to marry each other. She wants that too—"

"And why shouldn't she have it?" Boyd demanded and got out of the rocking chair, taking my part. "She's his wife. No sense your going around wearing that ring, Alice, perfectly silly—"

"All right, Boyd, you asked for it!" Tom left Alice and strode over to Boyd. "Now get out, go home. You're tired and not funny!"

Suddenly Alice came over to Boyd. She slid her arm through his, and to my amazement she smiled at him. "You've had a bad time today, Boyd. I'm sorry—come on, we'll go home."

Boyd gave me another surprise. He stopped grinning, and his eyes narrowed in a look of sly cunning. He withdrew his arm. "Oh, no, you don't."

"Now, Boyd, come with me." Alice reached for his arm again, and this time he slid behind the chair.

"No, you don't," he repeated. "Nothing doing. I'm never going to marry anybody again."

Then Alice drew from me reluctant admiration. She simply

99

walked around to Boyd and grasped his arm above the elbow in an efficient and obviously painful way, for Boyd winced. She said to Tom, coolly, "I'll see to him," and marched Boyd out of the cottage as neatly as any drill sergeant might have done.

Tom stared after them, stared at me for a moment, sat down on the sofa and gave me another surprise by beginning to laugh. He laughed and he laughed; he tried to say something to me and laughed again.

I got the bottle of whiskey from the cupboard and went to the kitchen, where I poured him a generous drink. By the time I'd got ice and water and brought it to Tom he had stopped, although he still looked a little shaken.

"Thanks."

"What were you laughing at?"

"I don't know. Really. That is—oh, the way she took Boyd out. Like a policeman."

I said, meanly, "You've always admired efficiency."

"Well, but—poor old Boyd."

"Poor old Boyd was good and drunk."

"It's my fault. It's been a ghastly day. I managed to get some whiskey for him and he needed it. But you know Boyd. He's no drinker, so it went to his head. He'll be all right."

Certainly Alice was all right, Alice had conquered. Tom still had not had a straight talk with Alice and she still had her diamond, which was beginning to be a symbol.

I sat down on the sofa beside Tom. I was very glad that he was back again, close to me. But I couldn't say to him: Alice thinks it was murder, and perhaps, just perhaps, she has reason to know that it was murder. She didn't like Mildred, not really; they were not really friends. I think—but I don't know, I only think—that Mildred hinted at some hold she had over Alice, something Alice did not want you to know, when Mildred said that Alice might not make a very good wife. Alice is very strong. Alice came here—perhaps because she is puzzled; that's what she said. But perhaps she came to question me because she wanted to know whether or not anyone suspects her. She knew about the skateboard.

Yet I didn't really suspect Alice of murder; I only suspected her of some hidden friction with Mildred. And I couldn't have said any of all that to Tom.

He rose and said he'd get me a drink. Then he saw the skateboard. "What's that?"

And I couldn't tell Tom that the skateboard he had in his hand had jolted me momentarily into black logic which ruthlessly said that Tom had murdered Mildred and that he threatened my own life. I couldn't even beg him to forgive me. I looked at his puzzled face and his dark head and his hands turning the skateboard, and I loved him and I said flatly, "It's a skateboard. A child's toy. It was on the top of the long flight of steps, the forty steps we used to call them. And there's a hammer upstairs again. It was on my dressing table."

So he looked at the skateboard and listened while I told him about it; then he went upstairs and looked at the hammer and listened. The room reeked of lilac scent. I showed him the chunk of wet sand which by then had dried a little. Finally he led the way downstairs again, carrying the hammer. He put it away in a kitchen drawer under some folded tea towels and said rather absently that the handle might but probably wouldn't show fingerprints.

"Have you had anything to eat?" I asked at last.

"Oh, sure. At the airport—"

"I'll scramble some eggs."

He followed me into the kitchen. We scrambled eggs and made toast and hot chocolate and I told him again, as he questioned me, in detail about the skateboard, the hammer and the little chunk of wet sand. I even told him that Alice had been on the porch above, had seen me fall, had seen me pick up something, had come to the cottage and explored until she found the skateboard—easily because there was really no other place to hide it.

"Boyd couldn't have put the skateboard there," Tom said. "He couldn't have left the hammer upstairs. He was with me all day. Sister, we've got to tell the sheriff the whole thing, the truth, exactly as it happened."

"No! No, Tom, no."

"This settles it. It's not fair to the sheriff not to tell him. And it's not fair to Boyd, to me, to you. I can't feel that Boyd

101

killed Mildred. I believe we were wrong about that. But she was killed, and whoever did it is at large and apparently is threatening you. Boyd is not the only person on the island. There are the two Bronsons, strangers. I don't know anything about them. There are you and me and the Sahib and John and—well, and Alice." He paused and said, "Not a likely list. But the sheriff ought to be told the truth."

"You've forgotten Leaf."

"Oh, yes. Well, all right, add Leaf to the list."

"The sheriff will say you did it. You had a motive. He'll arrest you. There'll be a trial. No, Tom—"

It was going to be the same old argument. Tom said, "Wait till morning. We'll see."

So I went upstairs, leaving Tom to clear up the dishes. I got out blankets and a pillow from the tiny linen cupboard and slid them down the stairs. He heard the soft thump and came out from the kitchen. "What are you going to do about the hammer and the skateboard?" I asked.

"I don't know. I've been looking at that hammer, but it's just a hammer. All sorts of tools have collected around the place over the years. I don't see any way of identifying it. But it's the kind of evidence the sheriff ought to have—"

"Tom, *don't* give it to the sheriff!"

"We'll see," he said again.

All right, we'll see, I thought, for I wasn't giving up yet. "You still haven't talked to Alice. She's still got your diamond."

He looked up at me then, puzzled. "Do you really want that diamond?"

"Well—yes."

"But I'll get you a diamond if you want it. Or a sapphire. Actually, I've always liked sapphires, but Alice wanted a diamond."

I didn't say anything. He said, frowning, "Seems funny women should care about a diamond."

"All women are funny about diamonds," I said, and flounced into my bedroom and shut the door hard. When it was too late it occurred to me that I had never once thought of my resolve to tell Alice the facts of my marriage. For a moment I was rather pleased because I had conquered my better nature, but only for a moment; Alice would have to know the facts sooner or later.

Gradually the little sounds from below diminished. Somehow it added to my sense of rage when I heard the thump of the sofa springs and then utter silence and I was sure that Tom was sound asleep. At the same time I felt safe.

The next morning the hammer disappeared again, but in an accountable way. Tom was gone when I got downstairs. The hammer and the skateboard were gone too, so I was sure that he had taken them. I wondered what he was going to do with them. Wally Rutherford arrived at the cottage door as I was finishing my coffee and wishing that I had not talked to Tom like a shrew the night before. The door was open and I watched Wally coming along the path; he stopped in the doorway, hitched up his jeans and said, "Hello."

"Hello, Wally."

He gave his pants another hitch. He was brown, skinny and had a magic touch with anything mechanical. "They said you wanted me to overhaul the Ark."

Boyd or Tom had called the old cabin cruiser Noah's Ark for so long that everybody else called her the Ark, though she had a real name, *The Flying Dutchman*, which was faded out, and a number which Wally kept painted black. I said blankly, "Why, no, Wally—"

"That's what they said. I was up to the Cape. The girl in the office wrote it out. Mrs. Esseven phoned to overhaul the Ark —that was Friday," Wally said. "I guess—why, I guess that was Mrs. Boyd that phoned and left the message."

I felt a queer kind of coldness over my skin. It hadn't occurred to me before then that now I was the only Mrs. Esseven. Mildred wouldn't have liked that. I said, as steadily as I could, "Yes, it must have been."

"Yes." He eyed me, and whatever lively curiosity there was in his light blue eyes was effectually concealed. "Well, I guess now I'm here I might as well take a look at her. But you can't take that boat out, Mrs. Esseven, not till she's been overhauled."

I hesitated. "I really don't think we want to take her out, Wally."

There was always a fine line drawn about titles between

Piney Point and the island. Boyd and Tom and Wally had played on the Piney Point softball team when they were young; they had sailed together and had tinkered over the runabout and the Ark's engines together. Wally would never have said Mr. Esseven when referring to Tom or Boyd. But he spoke of Mildred stiffly as Mrs. Esseven, and the Sahib was always Mr. Esseven and the sheriff was always the sheriff. I had a notion that Wally had brooded over my new status and decided to try Mrs. Esseven instead of Sister.

Apparently at that point he discarded the Mrs. Esseven. He said, more naturally, "Haven't wished you happiness yet, Sister. I sure do, though," and shook hands with me.

"Thank you, Wally."

"Not that it was much of a surprise to me," he said coolly. "Well, I'll just take a look at the Ark."

He had already started off down the path, and he was out of sight before a horrifying thought struck me. I knew that Mildred's body had lain all Friday night in the dinghy and I could see again the dreadfully damaged head; there might be some trace of its resting place. I ran after Wally, but he had already reached the boathouse and was inside it when I came running across the beach.

The boathouse was as clumsy and old-fashioned as the Ark. The sensible thing to do with the Ark would have been to have her put up during winters in the Piney Point boatyard. It was never done. The boathouse itself had probably been built expressly to accommodate the Ark. It was a high, shedlike building, weathered and damp. Wally had already opened the door and was standing just inside surveying the Ark. The padlock on the door was still clinging to the hasp, which had been torn out. Wally said, "Somebody sure jerked out that hasp."

I said nothing. The water side of the boathouse was not simply an open space, making a slip for the boats; there were two big doors across it. Wally walked along the little platform and contrived to reach the bolt. The doors creaked, then the gloom in the boathouse lightened as the doors opened. The Ark lay there, wallowing a little in the water and looking extremely uninviting.

She had come with the island. Nobody knew how old she

was. Wally came back, swung his legs over the teakwood rail, opened the cabin hatch and glanced inside; then he went lightly up the tiny ladder to the wheelhouse. But the dinghy was gone.

The sheriff said coolly, behind me, "What are you looking for?"

I seemed to swallow my heart with a gulp. "I didn't know you were on the island."

"Oh, sure. We brought Boyd's boat back from Marshtown. Tied up at Boyd's pier." He eyed me and said, "Funny, the dinghy for the Ark seems to be missing. I looked for it Saturday. Looked all over the Ark, Saturday, as a matter of fact."

chapter 10

He wouldn't have missed that. The dinghy was comparatively new; the Sahib had bought it as a safety precaution when Tom and Boyd and I spent our days around the boats. It had no engine, only oars; it was small and usually swung from davits behind the wheelhouse.

I didn't know what to say, so I said nothing. There was a hoarse and reluctant grunt from the Ark. The sheriff said, "Is Wally trying to start the engine?"

"I suppose so."

The grunt died away, and Tom came up behind the sheriff. "What are you doing?"

The sheriff shrugged. "Looking at the old boat. How's the Sahib?"

"He had another attack this morning. Not bad, but I've sent for the doctor."

Again I didn't know whether it was a real attack or a fake one, but something about Tom's manner made me think that it was a fake one, for he looked frustrated and angry. Then I guessed why, for the sheriff said, "Too bad, Tom. Well, I'll just go and have a word with Boyd."

The sheriff wouldn't have spoken like that if Tom had told him all we knew about Mildred's murder. So I was sure that Tom had told the Sahib that he intended to tell the sheriff everything he knew and that his uncle had chosen his strongest weapon, a heart attack, in order to stop him.

Tom said, "Boyd is at his house, I think. Anything you can talk to me about? Boyd had a hard time yesterday."

"Yes, I know. He was just getting up when we brought his boat in this morning."

The sheriff strolled out of the boathouse. Wally shouted down, "Hey, Tom. I better take her over to Piney Point."

Tom looked up, startled. "Wally!"

"Mrs. Esseven told me to get the Ark in shape."

"Mrs. Esseven? Oh." I saw comprehension and something like horror come over Tom's face as he realized that Wally referred to Mildred.

I said quickly, "She might as well get an overhaul, Tom."

"Of course, yes, all right, Wally. Anything you say."

Wally's grunt sounded like that of the engine. The sheriff squinted at the sun, said, "See you later," and started up the steps. Tom looked after him. "The sheriff's checking on the fuel in Boyd's boat," he said tonelessly. "Trying to get Boyd to tell him exactly when and where he last fueled up."

"What about the Sahib?"

"Oh, I told him I'd decided we had to tell the sheriff the truth. So—" He shrugged. "And I can't tell whether it's real or faked. Anyway, I put the hammer in the safe in his room. I hid the skateboard in my room."

"You didn't tell him about them?"

"No, how could I? As soon as I opened my mouth he guessed that I'd made up my mind to talk to the sheriff. He began to pant and gasp, and I swear, Sister, he turned blue. At least it looked that way. I don't know how he does it."

"Maybe it's real—"

"That's what I always think. By the time the doctor gets here he'll have had time to pretend to recover—or maybe really recover. I don't know."

"He'd better not be alone. I'll go—"

"Alice is there," Tom said.

She would be there: the lady of the house. I saw the sheriff's head emerge from behind green brambles and some flowering red ramblers along the steps. John's head appeared beside him, and they paused to exchange a few words.

Tom said, "The sheriff ought to be told. I know I'm right."

107

"No, Tom, no." Every time I looked at or thought of the sheriff and what he would do once he heard the full story, I turned cold; literally, right there in the warm sunlight, I could feel a kind of chill crawl up my back.

Wally came down the ladder. "I can't get to work on the Ark for a few days, Tom. Maybe not till the end of the week. All right with you?"

"Oh, of course, Wally. There's no hurry."

"I'll be going, then. Say, what's happened to her dinghy? Can't see it anywhere."

"Her—why, I don't know." Tom did know or guessed, and I could see the knowledge hide itself quickly in his eyes. "Maybe Boyd's got it over at his pier."

"Maybe," Wally said. "Oh, I forgot. Congratulations." He shook hands with Tom, and said again, "Not that it's much of a surprise to anybody really. You and Sister . . . Well, congratulations."

We had all moved out onto the pier, and the staccato of an approaching outboard thudded toward us. Wally squinted out to sea, said, "Here's Mrs. Mapping—" made a kind of salute in Tom's direction and boarded his own sleek motorboat as Mrs. Mapping, with Henrietta beside her, roared up to the pier and stopped. Mrs. Mapping neatly hoicked up the outboard motor and hopped dextrously onto the pier. Henrietta followed, staring at Tom and me. Mrs. Mapping shook hands briskly and said something about good wishes, and Henrietta shook hands too, rather damply.

"I heard you went with Boyd to the funeral," Mrs. Mapping said to Tom.

They knew everything that happened on the island. Mrs. Mapping, I was sure, would have gone to the stake for us; I wasn't so sure about Henrietta. In any event, they started up the steps and passed John coming on down. Wally's motorboat started off smoothly as John crossed the beach toward us. "The sheriff wants to know what happened to the dinghy," he said to Tom.

"What did you do with it?"

"I rowed out to the east end of the island early Saturday morning," John said. "It was not quite light, very misty. I was

108

sure nobody could see me. I'd planned to sink the dinghy out there. But all at once the sun came up and I was afraid I might be seen. So I just shoved her in among the reeds and left her there. We've got to sink her, Tom. The sooner the better. It—" John glanced at me and said, "It shows. They can have it analyzed—"

"All right," Tom said shortly. "I'll see about it."

"Why, you young fool, the sheriff is here! The doctor's on his way. It's broad daylight—"

"Where's the dinghy?"

"I'd have to show you. Tom, we'll have to wait, we can't go out there now—"

"I'll go," I said. "I know that end of the island. Nobody will see me. I'll find the dinghy and row it into one of those little inlets that's full at high tide and hide her. Maybe I can manage to sink her—I'll try."

Tom said, frowning, "Does anybody know when it's high tide today?"

Nobody knew; nobody had paid any attention to the tides lately.

"We can't wait," I said. "Can you remember exactly where you left her, John?"

"I can find her. Here's the doctor—"

We turned as we heard the regular beat of a motorboat again, and watched it approach the pier. The doctor was wearing sun glasses; his son, home from the university for vacation, was at the wheel. I said rapidly, "I'll see about the dinghy, Tom. John will go with me. You'll have to go with the doctor to the Sahib."

The doctor seemed to eye us glumly from behind his dark glasses; the boy at the wheel waved jauntily as he brought the boat in with a swirl.

John said, "I phoned to the office. Told them none of us would be in today. They'd had no news of Mildred's death yet. I told them it was an accident. Come on, Sister." We walked on across the beach slowly, as if we had agreed to hide the urgency of our errand.

The east end of the island was deceptive to a casual observer; it looked perfectly flat and very green. It was green,

109

but it was anything but flat owing to the unexpected little ridges and sudden inlets of mud or water. Most of it was marshland, though there was an occasional outcropping of small rocks or pebbles. Reeds and marsh grass were everywhere, deceptive in their look of green flatness. Some of the reeds were very tall, breast-high or higher, and in late summer had purple and brown plumes; some of the grass was short and could conceal nobody.

We set out along the path to the cottage and veered through the stand of pines which petered away to swamp and reeds. We walked among the reeds, though there were a few strips of higher and firmer paths which made for easier going. We had played there, Tom and Boyd and I; it was ideal for Red Indians and pirates.

The sun beat down upon us; the reeds were so tall that they almost covered our heads and shut out any breeze. When John stepped into mud for the third time and pulled his foot out with an angry mutter I told him that I thought I knew a way, and after some time spent getting my bearings and wishing the sun did not blaze down so hotly, I found it; once it had been almost a path. The ground was just a little higher and firmer than the surrounding marshland. I brushed reeds aside and could see the lighthouse on Crab Island, which stood out starkly against that blazing blue sky.

When I released the sharp-edged reeds they clashed together and closed suffocatingly around me. John must have hidden the dinghy close to the water's edge, but the shoreline along that end of the island was irregular and confusing. We had groped around through the reeds for some time when I called back to him, "Where do you think you hid the dinghy?"

He was panting and sounded harried by the heat and the reeds. "Toward the left, I think. I'm not sure of my directions."

"Take a look at Crab Island. That will orient you."

I could hear the brushing of the reeds and turned to peer back. John was farther behind me than I had believed, standing on tiptoe, his face pink with the heat, his gray hair limp and his gray mustache bristly. He shaded his eyes from the sun. Crab Island was forbiddingly clear; I felt as if we were under observation, though the lighthouse keeper certainly had other things to do.

"I don't know," John said. "North, I think."

"We'll have to work down nearer the shoreline."

"All right. Oh, here's a rock." John picked up a jagged, heavy stone. "Should we gather enough to sink her?"

"No," I said. "We'd better knock a hole in her."

John hefted the rock. "I'll take it along then. I can't see it, but there's an inlet about a hundred yards further north, isn't there?"

"There are little trickles of inlets everywhere." I was hot and tired and also afraid that at any moment I might hear the thud of a motorboat, the sheriff's or a Coast Guard boat. All at once the reeds changed; they were thicker but lower, so our heads were now visible.

John peered toward the north. "I think the dinghy's over there—stay here and I'll find out. I'll wave at you to come if I find her."

"All right."

The island was small, but now it seemed very large, and the reeds and inlets were confusing. As I watched John's head going along through the reeds I suddenly heard the sound I'd been dreading, the throb of a motorboat. Either the doctor or the sheriff was leaving, and both of them had sharp eyes. I whirled around, but couldn't see a boat yet; it was behind the growth of pines. I called after John. "John! Duck! There's a boat—" But apparently he had already heard the boat, for he had disappeared. I ducked down, too, at once. The muddy patch beside me smelled of salt and mire. The reeds closed over my head, making a slanting green curtain. I thought of the times when I had crouched down exactly like that when we were playing Red Indian. Somehow I was always the scalpee, perhaps because I was younger and a girl, or perhaps merely because I had longer hair and thus was a more alluring prize for the scalper. In any event, the pretense had been so vivid that while I knew perfectly well that only Boyd or Tom was stalking me and watching for the slightest motion in the reeds which would disclose my whereabouts, I always worked myself up into such a state of terror that my heart thumped. It

111

was so clear a memory that I could almost hear Tom or Boyd brushing through the reeds somewhere near me, pushing them cautiously aside, scrunching stealthily upon some spot of small stones, coming nearer.

I could no longer hear the motorboat, so I stood up. I couldn't see John, but when I turned, there was Nadine, standing at the edge of the reeds, her red hair glowing in the sun, her dark glasses winking.

"Lost something?" she called to me cheerily.

I looked quickly out toward Piney Point; the day was so clear after the storm of the previous day that I could see the doctor's motorboat, now almost at the Piney Point wharf. So the Sahib's attack, if attack it was, had not been serious; if it had been, the doctor would not have gone so soon. I turned back to Nadine. I must get her too-observant green eyes out of that dangerous spot at once. I had a dreadful notion that at any moment John would stand up and wave at me and Nadine would see it and ask questions. I crashed through the remaining reeds to Nadine. "I'm going back to the cottage."

"Were you out for a walk?"

"Yes."

"I saw you and John dodging around among the reeds as if you were playing Indian. Oh, there's John." I whirled around and saw John's head moving above the reeds, down nearer the shore. He didn't turn, and I said, "Let's go back. It's frightfully hot here in the sun."

"Oh, well, all right. If it's a secret."

I led the way and Nadine followed, but she was curious. "Where did John go?"

"I haven't the faintest idea." This happened to be altogether too accurate. I only hoped he'd find the dinghy.

We approached the shady strip of scraggly pines, and for an instant I had a fantastic notion that one of the pines had moved very quickly before my eyes. I looked hard and saw that it wasn't a pine tree, but Leaf Trace; in that heat his wiry little figure was clad in a weird combination of tight green pants and brown sweater, and as I watched he slid behind more pines and disappeared into their green and brown shadows.

Nadine said rather sharply, "Who was that?"

"Leaf. Greenleaf Trace."

"What's he sneaking around like that for?"

"Oh, I don't know! It doesn't matter."

"I see. All right. I know when I'm told to shut up. But it might interest you to know that Boyd and my husband are having a long talk."

There was something significant in her voice. In one stabbing instant, I knew exactly what she meant.

We were in the light shade cast by a scraggly pine tree. Facing Nadine, I could also see the low, flat stretch of the island, which looked so calmly level and was in fact so treacherously irregular, the sea glittering beyond it.

I could not see John but I saw Tom. He was rising from a thick clump of reeds off at my left. It was not far from the place where I had crouched down, all at once overtaken by the same fantasy of terror which had caught me as a child.

Nadine's black glasses swiveled around. She cried hoarsely, her voice sounding almost like a marsh bird's, "Oh, Tom! There you are again!" She turned to me. "What goes on here? I've been watching. You and John and Tom all dodging around in the grass, or whatever you call that green stuff. Even that little Greenleaf Trace is sneaking around. Are you playing hide and seek?"

Tom came toward us, thrusting through the reeds. His dark hair shone in the sun; his shirt showed patches of dampness. He wiped off his forehead with the back of one hand and grinned at me. "Still midges down there. And mosquitoes. Did you get bitten?"

"How long have you been there?" I asked. In the same instant I could almost feel Nadine's ears perk up and sharpen.

Tom was aware of Nadine's sharp interest too, for he only shrugged and said, "Not long. Let's get out of the sun."

We all strolled into the strip of pines, and I said, "Tom, Nadine says that Boyd and her husband are having a long talk."

Tom stopped dead-still and looked at Nadine. Her big black glasses winked in the sun. She nodded. "At Boyd's house. Alice is there with them. George knows nothing of publishing. I really wish you'd stop Boyd."

Tom turned slowly to me. "But he wouldn't."

"I don't know. Tom, I don't know. I'm afraid he would."

.........chapter 11.................................

There was a long pause. Little heat waves seemed to dance beyond Tom's shoulder, among the tall green reeds. At last Tom said, "I'll wait for John. Will you go along to Boyd's house, Sister, and—and see what's going on? I'll be there in a few minutes."

I nodded. Tom meant that he'd find and get rid of the dinghy.

I said to Nadine, "Let's take the south shore path. It's over this way. It's easier—"

It was also longer than the way across the beach and around the big house, but we had the shade of pines some of the way and also I could glance back toward Tom and John. I restrained myself until we reached the path, when I knew that in another moment the reedy, miry long finger of the island would be out of sight, and then permitted myself to look back. Neither Tom nor John was visible. Nadine said, dryly, "I think they'll find it all right."

I dared to say, "Find what?" and even laughed a little and shaded my eyes, for the sea, close beside us now, was glaringly bright.

"Whatever you're all looking for. Although I really thought that Tom was trying to find you. He was sneaking around, moving very cautiously through the reeds. Once in a while he'd put up his head just a little to look over the place; then he'd lower it again. I could see the reeds move, though."

We came out on the path. Here the outcropping of rocks

upon which the big house stood began and climbed slowly upward. Here, too, there was a slow and usually mild surf, breaking in curling white spray against the rocks. The sun was full upon us, but there was a light, cooling breeze from the water.

Nadine took off her dark glasses, wiped them on a shirt tail and put them back on again. It was just then, as she adjusted the black glasses, that a curious thought struck me. It was as if it had lingered along for some moments at the edge of my consciousness. I'd had an absurd notion that somebody had been stalking me through the reeds. Tom, Nadine had said, was following me.

Logic died hard. Tom was the only person I knew of who had a real reason for disposing of my testimony forever.

I felt odd, a little light-headed really, as if the heat among the reeds had been dizzying. Nadine said abruptly, "Do you want to sit down?"

"It's only the sun."

I would not listen to the preposterous suggestion of logic. Tom wouldn't have prowled through the reeds after me like that. Nadine said, in a perfectly cool and conversational way, "Of course Alice is egging Boyd on."

"What—"

"To sell the business."

I stared at Nadine, who marched on beside me. "Alice?"

"Oh, my child, look at the facts of life."

"But Alice has nothing to do with the business." I remembered the scene in the living room the night Mildred was killed. "Alice said she never intended to have anything to do with the business even after she and Tom were married."

"But she and Tom are not married," Nadine said neatly, "and if you've got the sense God gave a goose, they never will be. No, the whole point is that Alice needs money right now."

"Alice! But she can't—"

"But she can. She's in debt up to her ears and overdrawn at her bank. If you want to know how I know it, it's because I looked through the desk in the bedroom she's using. Stuffed to the brim with bills."

I opened my mouth and shut it again. Nadine said rather

grimly, "When anybody makes a play for George, I try to find out just how serious a bore she's going to be to me. I find out everything I can about her. So naturally I looked at her letters. Of course, Alice is working on Boyd, too."

I was not really surprised by this. Boyd had seen it coming and said so with startled, determined candor the night before. I said, "Boyd wouldn't think of marriage again." Suddenly the fact that within the past three days Boyd had become available to a designing female and the reason why came before me as if it had a presence. Mildred's head and her black, wet hair seemed to flash across the glittering, glaring sea. "It's too soon," I said to Nadine. "It's too soon."

"Not too soon for Alice. Boyd or George, anybody to support her in the style she likes. She's got to get money from somewhere."

Alice hadn't really liked Mildred; she had not threatened Alice in so many words, yet I had had a curious impression that Mildred knew something which Alice hoped that Tom would not know. I could hear Mildred's scornful yet knowing voice. Mildred had said, "Perhaps your bride, Tom, won't be such a good wife either."

I said abruptly, "Did Mildred know this about Alice?"

Nadine considered it. "I should think so," she said in a matter-of-fact way. "I rather think Mildred didn't miss much. Naturally, Alice wouldn't have wanted Tom to know that she would have seized the first man who came along with money, as I think she would. Still, I must say you have to give Alice credit for the fact that it apparently never occurred to her that anybody would bother to read her letters. Yes, I think Alice is basically quite a nice woman. But quite decent women will fight for their lives."

We came around a curve of rocks and pines, and Boyd's house, shining with new gray paint and red geraniums, lay before us. It was a copy of a Maine cottage; it was so perfect in every detail that it proclaimed its falsity. It was a cold gray; it had small windows; it had a great chimney; it had flowering plants and green vines everywhere. There was a scrap of lawn, which was bright green. The windows sparkled. There was a bow to modernity in the way of a terrace on the sea side of the house; the terrace was carefully outlined, too, in boxes of bright red geraniums. Alice and George Bronson sat on the terrace, and Boyd was pacing around the flagstones, his dark head bent. It was shady there, for tall pines grew at each end. Down below us, Boyd's sleek new cabin cruiser rocked lightly at a tiny pier. Everything was spick and span and hadn't the faintest look of having grown there or, as a matter of fact, of ever having been lived in. It was like a photograph, made up for the purpose. I could almost see the legend: "Maine cottage by the sea."

Alice saw us, and simply looked without moving. She was very beautiful, with her long hair falling almost to her shoulders, and she looked very young. Bronson was clad in gray, again perfectly tailored; his shirt was monogrammed in a darker shade of gray. He watched us too as Boyd went on pacing.

Bronson rose as we came up the two flagstones that made steps. He said good morning to me. I greeted him and Boyd, who gave me an absent look, and Alice, who adjusted the belt of her shorts and said nothing. As always she was perfectly turned out in pink, pink trimly-fitting shirt and shorts. I was beginning to loathe rosebud-pink. She also, which was rather surprising, had a gold ribbon around her long hair, tying it back, and, more surprising, wore gold sandals. Her legs were slender and perfectly tanned; the gold ribbon and the gold sandals were out of place. Usually everyone on the island wore the simplest of country clothes and shoes. Once one of our authors had mistaken the warning that the Sahib gave everybody about how we lived very simply on the island, and she had arrived in full bush attire, bringing a sleeping bag with her. It was quite natural in a way, for the author had just written a book about a hunting safari she had undertaken, but Mrs. Mapping was very indignant when she stumbled over the sleeping bag on the veranda where the author insisted upon sleeping and then the author was indignant too. The Sahib was a little ruffled himself; his sense of decorum was upset. But for a time afterward Tom and Boyd and I got considerable pleasure out of imitating as best we could wild beast noises within the hearing of the Sahib, until he called us all into the hell room.

It seemed strange to remember all this while standing there on the terrace, with the brilliant red geraniums around and Boyd pacing up and down and Alice with her undeniably good legs gracefully disposed and George Bronson just blank and secretive. It also seemed strange to stand on the terrace which Mildred had planned and for which she had chosen the chairs and tables, all of them in cast iron painted white. The Sahib called them cemetery chairs—as, indeed, I believe they once were. He didn't like Mildred's taste in furnishing the house either; kitchen antiques, he had said scornfully, eying a cobbler's bench turned into a cocktail table. When he saw the hand-pegged floors he said sourly that it must have cost Boyd an ugly penny. Now, looking at some magenta petunias in what once must have been a watering trough, I felt a miserable wave of pity for Mildred. She hadn't deserved to die like that.

I also felt a reluctant kind of pity for Alice; I hadn't a doubt that Nadine was right. Alice could wear her beautiful clothes and air her elegances, but it couldn't be very pleasant to be desperately in need of money. But then she moved her hand so that Tom's diamond flashed, and I hardened my heart and listened to what she and George Bronson were saying. It wasn't much; indeed, it was so trivial and flat a conversation about how changeable the weather was on the island (as in fact it always was hot and sunny, hot and humid, cold and foggy; nobody could predict its sudden whims), that I knew at once the gyrations of the weather had been seized upon when Nadine and I arrived.

Boyd ran a hand through his hair, then broke in, speaking directly to Bronson, "I'll think about it. That's all I can say right now."

Alice tossed back her hair and smiled over my shoulder. I turned to see Tom and John walking along the path toward the house. Tom was looking troubled, his eyes on Boyd; John was plodding along behind him and paused to wipe his face with a handkerchief. Boyd saw them too.

Obviously Boyd had almost decided to sell the business, had

all but agreed to Bronson's offer; I knew that when I saw the look on his face. There was a certain flashing gaiety in Boyd's smile, a certain very direct way of eying anybody, a certain air of ease which he always had employed when he felt guilty about anything in the world.

I wasn't sure whether Tom recognized it or not; probably he did and probably John did. But if so, neither of them showed it. As they came up on the terrace Boyd flashed his smile, said he'd get some cold drinks and disappeared at once. Tom went into the house after him.

I wanted to be sure that the dinghy was hidden, so I told John that the Sahib wanted to see him. The facility with which I was beginning to lie was really unpleasant; I had an uneasy feeling that sometime soon conscience was going to rise up and smite. But just then Tom was more important to me than anything. John strolled away with me, and Nadine called, "*Ciao*" after us, which confused me a little, for first I thought chow dog and then I thought chow lunch, and only belatedly arrived at "Ciao" Italian. Alice didn't bother to say anything, and Bronson's tiger eyes were narrow and alert, watching the door into the house where Boyd and Tom had disappeared.

I hoped that Tom could talk Boyd out of his temptation to sell the business. But first I had to find out what had happened to the dinghy and what the sheriff was doing. We walked around the west end of the island; the path sloped upward a little, but it was an easy walk to the big house. John knew what I wanted to know. "It's all right," he said. "I found it. Tom and I sunk her in a little inlet Tom knew about. She's completely covered with mud and marsh grass. The sheriff would have to cover every inch of the island to find her."

It sounded horrible, as if we were concealing a body. "Was there much—I mean, could the sheriff have found any evidence—"

"Oh, I suppose so," John said grumpily. "All these new-fangled ways of analyzing the smallest bloodstain. That's why I rowed around and hid the dinghy early Saturday morning before we called the sheriff."

We came out onto the steps below the porch just then. Evidently somebody had telephoned from the office, and Henrietta came hurrying to tell us. Her bright black eyes were greedier than usual, and while John went to the telephone she asked me what room in the big house I wanted prepared for Tom and me. I said shortly that for the moment we would stay in the cottage. Henrietta looked disappointed, but rallied and said that there was something she wanted to tell the sheriff about and did I think the sheriff would mind.

"Of course not. Tell him."

"Well, it's something that happened in Piney Point—" There was an excited gleam in her eyes, so I took it that whatever had happened in Piney Point appealed to her love of drama. I told her, repressively, to think it over just as Mrs. Mapping flashed out of the house. "Now then, Henrietta, you let Sister alone. If she and Tom want to spend their honeymoon in the cottage, what's wrong with that?"

"But Sister's mistress of the house now, Ma. Seems to me she ought to take her rightful place."

"Get along with the dusting," her mother said, and Henrietta sighed and vanished inside the house again as Mrs. Mapping gave me a very sharp look. "You want I should call you Mrs. Esseven, now?"

"Good heavens, no."

"It's fitting."

"Now listen, Mrs. Mapping—"

"All right, all right. But that Mildred, she was Mrs. Esseven. Not that I should say a word against her. She's dead and gone, poor soul."

I said yes and that I thought Tom and I would have lunch in the cottage.

"There's always plenty of cold things left over for Monday lunch," she said absently, verifying my suspicion that she planned it that way. "Now, Sister, there's something I've got to say."

I knew what was coming. Mrs. Mapping had had a very firm hand in bringing up all three of us. I said, "But it happened very suddenly, you see—"

"That makes no difference. You ought to have had it out with that Alice first."

120

"Well, I know," I said wearily. "I know, but—but that's the way it happened."

She gave me another sharp look, far too sharp. "There isn't anything wrong, is there?"

"Wrong?"

"You know what I mean. That Mildred—seems a queer sort of accident to me. Everybody's talking, but my advice to you, Sister, is don't you take any notice. You or Tom or Boyd. You just go straight along the way you always have. Let the sheriff fidget around all he wants to—" She paused, and said with perfect knowledge, "The gas in Boyd's boat checked out all right as far as they could figure it out."

I think I said, "Oh."

Mrs. Mapping said, "They measured before they brought the boat back from Marshtown. Got Boyd to say where last he had fueled and then checked with the attendant there. Unless Boyd got some fuel somewhere else, he couldn't have made the run from Marshtown to the island that night and then back to anchor at the cove near Marshtown." She paused again, not looking at me.

But of course Mrs. Mapping would know. Sometimes in my childhood I thought she had eyes that could see right straight through to anybody's thoughts. I didn't ask her how she knew about the fuel in Boyd's boat. She said, briskly, "Well, I've got work to do. You and Tom be sure you come up to the house to dinner tonight. Now mind me." She spoke exactly as if I were ten, and then her blue dress and neatly coiled gray hair swished back into the house.

John came out again. "It wasn't anything much from the office," he said. "Just the usual. Some author's galleys are too late for the printer. Somebody wants an advance by wire. Oh, they want a précis of the new Greenleaf Trace in time for the sales conference. Can you do it?"

"Yes."

"Somebody's coming to town, too. I told them that we couldn't have any visiting fireman here on the island just now. Told them to explain and get tickets for a musical. Sometimes I wonder how I got into this business." He looked thought-

121

fully out over the glittering sound. "Looks as if I might be getting out of it. Is Boyd going to sell to Bronson?"

"Tom will talk him out of it." I wasn't at all sure that anybody could talk Boyd out of anything. And Mrs. Mapping's relayed information about the fuel in Boyd's cruiser was nagging at me; if Boyd had not come quietly back to the island and killed Mildred, then—the same old troubled question—who *had* killed her?

John said, "The Sahib will have something to say too. I wish the sheriff would tell the Bronsons they could leave, so we could be rid of them."

"Perhaps he will," I said and started down the steps. This time I watched carefully every single step and held on to the railing. There were no more treacherous skateboards.

I went safely down the forty steps of the long flight, crossed the beach while the sun beat mercilessly down on my head and spent the rest of the day going from the sofa to a chair and back to the sofa, picking up Leaf's ominously thick manuscript and putting it down again, thinking and failing utterly to think in the right direction.

Henrietta brought down a basket of cold lunch; she would have lingered, but I told her that the cottage was already cleaned, and she went back to the big house. Tom did not come down to the cottage for lunch, and I was sure that he was wrestling out with Boyd the question of selling the business—except that nobody ever succeeded in getting Boyd to make a definite decision about anything until he was ready to do so.

Tom came in when the shadows through the pines were beginning to lengthen and turn blue. He looked tired, cross and worried. "Boyd won't say yes or no. We've been talking all day. Finally I got him to talk to the Sahib, and Boyd just agreed and agreed, but I don't like the way he looks. I'm sorry I didn't get here for lunch."

"That's all right. Mrs. Mapping thinks we ought to go to the big house to dinner."

"Yes, all right. I'll clean up. Oh, by the way, the fuel in Boyd's boat—"

"I know, Mrs. Mapping told me."

He accepted this omniscience on Mrs. Mapping's part without comment. "So there we are," he said. "I suppose Boyd could have come here and then refueled somewhere. It would take days to run that down." He passed his hand wearily over his face, said, "Good Lord, I haven't shaved," and went upstairs.

Presently I went upstairs too and searched through the tiny closet, which didn't take long. I decided on a white, thin dress and red sandals and sweater, for the nights always turned chilly. Tom shouted at me when he finished with the bathroom, and it was impossible for me to entertain for an instant the notion that down in the reeds and the mud and the heat that morning Tom had stalked me in real life as he or Boyd had stalked me in play when we were young. Obviously, he had been trying to find the dinghy or John. All of us had been foolishly ducking about, trying to attract nobody's attention and almost getting in each other's way.

When I went downstairs Tom, fresh in dark slacks and a dark blue summer coat, had poured cocktails for us. We sat in the little living room and listened to the night sounds of sleepy birds and a few early locusts and watched the twilight come down. We felt a little heartened—at least I did, so heartened and sure of myself that I asked Tom why he had gone down to the marsh that morning.

He rose and went to mix more cocktails. I didn't really think that he had done so to avoid my eyes or my question; yet he seemed a little evasive. "Oh, I only thought of—well, that hammer, you know. The skateboard. All that. Another martini?"

"But John was with me."

He stirred the martinis more vigorously than the Sahib permitted martinis to be stirred. "Yes. Oh, look here, Sister," he said abruptly, "if Boyd didn't kill Mildred, who did? It always comes back to that. Somebody's been playing tricks with that hammer and a skateboard. I wanted to go with you, that's all. As soon as the doctor took a look at the Sahib, I knew the old man was all right, so I ran after you. I couldn't see either you or John, but I saw some of the reeds moving."

"I wish you'd told me it was you crawling around after me!

Tom, I told John that I had seen him that night in the runabout. Nobody pays any attention to those two people in the runabout. I think they were John and Boyd."

Tom stared at me. "Why did you tell John that? You said at first that it was too dark and foggy to see anybody."

The martini had given me false confidence. I told Tom the truth. "Because I had to know that Boyd was on the island."

There was a rather long pause—too long. His gray eyes were very dark, very intent, and saw too much. "It had to be me or Boyd, and you'd rather it were Boyd."

Suddenly I felt ashamed and miserable. "Yes, I suppose so."

Tom gave an odd exclamation of something like irritation. "Well, you needn't look as if you'd robbed a bank. You wouldn't be very smart if you didn't at some time think that perhaps Tom did kill her. You saw me. You saw that damned hammer actually in my hand. You knew I detested her. You'd heard our quarrel. You knew about the business. If you're going to cry, stop it."

"I married you, didn't I?"

"I made you marry me."

"That's not true—"

"It takes two to make a bargain like that. Sure, I had Boyd on my mind. I could see that once the sheriff got the idea of murder, it would be bad. Our marriage is the only thing the Sahib ever asked of me, that's true. But don't think I didn't have my own skin in mind, too. Do you think I wanted to see you on the witness stand, telling a jury about me and the hammer?"

"Tom, you didn't kill her." I was terribly intent and serious.

Tom eyed me for a moment. Then he grinned a little. "All right. I didn't. If that makes you feel any better. What did John say when you told him you had seen him in the runabout with Boyd?"

"He said I hadn't."

"That's what you said that night."

"Yes. Well, that's true. I couldn't see anybody. Only two cigarettes. But I did see those."

He finished the last drop in his glass and waited a moment,

124

frowning. "The fact is that everybody on the island is snooping around in a fumbling, clumsy way. Everybody, except whoever it was who killed Mildred, has got the idea that there's something wrong and is doing little private chores of investigating. Nobody admits it, sure. Nobody wants to get seriously involved in a murder investigation, sure. We can't go on like this! It's a job for the police and for the law and—oh, don't look at me like that. You know I'm right. Have you finished your cocktail? Then we'd better go to the big house."

So we went slowly up the flights of steps to the big house. There the fireworks started almost immediately.

The two Bronsons, both very elegant, George in a wine-red coat and blue slacks and Nadine in a matching wine-red dress which was simple and exquisite, were having martinis, too, on the porch when Tom and I came up the last flight of steps. Alice was there, in pink naturally, but this time a filmy and very feminine dress and high-heeled slippers. Leaf Trace sat hunched beside Bronson; he had dressed for dinner rather weirdly, for he wore a violently purple turtleneck sweater, which almost hid his little chin, and skin-tight black trousers. He was smoking a cigarette, which gave me a surprise, in a foot-long holder. Even John looked as if he'd made a bow to festivity; he wore a sagging, wrinkled red coat above his sagging, wrinkled tweed trousers. But the star of the evening was the Sahib, who coolly came down to dinner quite as if he'd never heard of a heart attack that very morning. Boyd had helped him, he said, and kissed my cheek.

Boyd toasted the bride. Everybody stood, Alice rather slowly, and I felt for a second as if they meant it and I *was* a bride. Tom put his arm around me unexpectedly, so I knew that he sensed my uneasiness; in fact, I felt an impostor, accepting the toasts and the good wishes. The dinner, I saw, was intended to be a courtesy to me.

At last the Sahib herded us into the house. "Mrs. Mapping and Henrietta promised to stay to give us dinner tonight," he said and fluffed up his white curls. "But I don't think we should keep them late." He finished off his rather strong drink and said, "Will you take my arm, my dear?"

I did, again feeling rather odd, for this little formality had

125

never been observed before. I also felt perfectly miserable when he escorted me to the table in the dining room, the others trailing after us, and pulled out the chair opposite his own. I swallowed hard and sat down.

The Sahib had reversed himself, like a weathervane, and was making it uncomfortably clear that for the time being at least, he expected me, not Alice, to act as the hostess of the house.

There was wine that night, too. The sparkling old wineglasses were at our plates. I glanced once at Alice; she was looking rather green, but it was only the effect of a green segment of the glass chandelier, its light falling directly upon her face. She sat between Tom and Boyd, and Tom's diamond glittered on her hand.

Leaf pulled two bottles of pills from a pocket under his purple sweater, put them beside his plate and looked at his watch. This drew a rather sharp look of disapproval from the Sahib, which Leaf saw.

"I have to take them," he said defensively. "I must follow my regimen. All the doctors say so."

"I didn't know that you smoked cigarettes, Leaf," Tom said.

"Only during June," Leaf sighed. "It seems that I may have asthma, too. These cigarettes are medicated." He looked at his watch again and popped a pill down his throat as the Sahib shuddered a little too visibly. However, he said nothing. As we all knew, there were nice authors and not so nice authors, but all of them had whims of iron and Leaf Trace was very whimsical.

It was the wine which set off the fireworks. Boyd had been drinking more than usual before dinner. He soon rose to replenish the wineglasses, in spite of an alert and threatening gleam in the Sahib's old eyes. Leaf refused the wine and Boyd's hand as if both were lethal, and Boyd laughed. He was holding the decanter in his hand when he made his announcement. He'd decided to sell the business to George Bronson, he said. He was sorry, he was very sorry if the Sahib and Tom didn't agree with him, but that was his decision. Indeed, he made quite a speech in which he attributed his reason for selling the business to his gratitude to the Sahib. "I owe everything to him," Boyd said. "So does Tom. People think of us as his sons. He's always treated us like sons. He even turned over the business to us, but while Tom and I try, the Sahib, naturally, still feels the anxieties and responsibilities of the business. He's not young. He's in poor health. Tom and I owe him freedom from financial cares during his declining years. The decision was mine to make and I've made it." He added that he hoped everybody would be very happy and that the company would flourish, and would we drink a toast to good old Georgie Bronson.

This was as close as I could come to exactly what he said. Tom had gone perfectly, stonily white.

Nobody moved. Boyd waited a moment and said, "We owe it to the Sahib to relieve him of business cares. That's what Mildred said, too." Something flashed into Boyd's eyes which was not exactly mischief or malice but was very sharp and probing. "Everybody says Mildred's death was an accident. I think somebody hit her over the head. But it wasn't me."

..........chapter 12..........................

The Sahib moved then. He struck the table with his hand so the glasses jumped. "Boyd! It was an accident! You can't sell the business. You want to sell for the money, not for me. I brought you up, Boyd. You were taught to be a reliable, honorable man. I trusted you." The Sahib's lips were blue.

Tom went quickly to Boyd. "Stop it. You're killing him."

Boyd glanced around the table, avoided the Sahib's eyes and simply walked out of the room. Tom followed him. For a moment I could hear their footsteps in the hall; then the front door closed with a bang.

Nadine said with her usual frankness, "Come along, George. This is a family row. Thank you very much for dinner," she added, apparently addressing the green and purple chandelier.

So they left, George Bronson very quietly, even stealthily. I thought parenthetically that if it had been Bronson stalking me that morning through the reeds, I'd never have known it; there would never have been the slightest quiver of a single reed.

John said to the Sahib, "Come on. I'll help you upstairs."

"No!" the Sahib said. "No!" We'll not let Boyd do this."

"All right," John said in a very tired way. "How are we going to stop him?"

"Ways," the Sahib said. "Ways. First thing we'll do is play for time. You'll have to draw up the papers. You can put all kinds of blocks in the way of a sale, hold it up as long as possible and give us time—"

128

John rose. "How can we keep Boyd from simply calling in some different lawyers, somebody we don't know? He's got a right to do as he pleases—" He stopped, for there was a commotion in the hall. Henrietta squealed, "Ooh, you kissed me!"

There was the unmistakable sound of baggage being thumped down, and a man's hearty voice bellowed, "My dream girl! Where's the family?"

Henrietta giggled and shot into the doorway, her cheeks red, and a man, vast, bearded, ruddy, calmly pushed her out of the way and advanced happily upon us. "Forgotten you invited me?" he boomed cheerfully.

It was Egbert Drippley (which was the name he signed to his contracts but not to his books), and his books sold. John pulled himself together first, came around the table in his dashing red coat and put out his hand. "Why, Egbert! No, we weren't expecting you, but of course—glad to see you. How did you get to the island? I didn't hear a boat."

During the last few moments none of us would have heard the crack of doom. Egbert caressed his beard. "Oh, I hired some boy at Piney Point to bring me here. Name was Wally something. No, no," he said to Mrs. Mapping, who had come hurriedly in from the pantry, before she could mention dinner. "I knew you'd be having dinner. I had mine on the train —early, but all right. No, no, don't bother with me. Well, now, you old scoundrel." He bustled along the table to shake hands with the Sahib. "How are you?"

The Sahib permitted his hand to be shaken and shot me a glance which plainly called for aid. I got up. "I'm terribly sorry, but there's been a death in the family—"

Egbert's thick eyebrows shot up. "What's that? Who?"

I said, "It was Boyd's wife. Mildred. Friday night. I'm sorry we didn't think to let you know." I reminded myself of everything I had heard of the care and feeding of authors, swallowed hard and said, "But of course you are welcome. We'll just take your bags up to a guest room—"

Egbert interrupted me. He couldn't tell us how sorry he was, barging in like this; he'd go straight back to town. No, no, he wouldn't think of staying overnight—too much bother altogether. He had a timetable; there was a train back to town in about an hour.

To do us justice, we did urge, the Sahib and John and I and even Mrs. Mapping, who had heard every word, and being accustomed to authors, knew just what to do. But in spite of his bluff manner Egbert had real tact; he couldn't have failed to see that he had arrived at the wrong time. He shook hands all around, even with Leaf, and Alice; he was sorry he couldn't see Boyd but he wouldn't intrude; would we give Boyd his sympathy? All this got him out into the hall, with the Sahib still sitting at the dining-room table; Alice sat there too, twiddling the diamond on her hand and smiling. John and I followed Egbert, and I said helplessly that we'd take him to Piney Point ourselves if he really insisted upon leaving.

John managed to bundle the two great bags Egbert had brought onto the porch and drew me aside. "You'd better find Tom. Let him take Egbert over in the runabout. The Sahib's looking a little bad. I'll get him upstairs."

Egbert overheard this and shook John's arm nearly out of its socket again and said that indeed he must see to the Sahib, the old pirate, we couldn't let anything happen to him, and that we'd find Tom ourselves, wherever he was.

Then he heaved up his two bags and started jauntily down the steps. John gave me a helpless look, much like the Sahib's, and not knowing what else to do, I followed the broad shoulders going down the steps before me.

It was full dark by now and rather cloudy, so there was no starlight. We came out on the beach; the light on the boathouse outlined its black shape as always. There was no sight of Tom and Boyd. I asked Egbert to wait for a moment while I went to find them, and I crossed the beach, through the pines, to the cottage. It was dark, so I knew that Tom and Boyd were not there. I assumed that they must be at Boyd's house, and it seemed unwise to interrupt their talk at that moment. The simplest way to get rid of Egbert was to take him to Piney Point myself. I went into the cottage, turned on lights and took the flashlight which I always kept on the mantel. Then I made my way back to Egbert, who was sitting on the step of the boathouse, smoking. He protested a little when I

130

led him out along the pier, shot my flashlight down into the runabout and said I couldn't find Tom but that I would take him to Piney Point.

"But, my dear—"

"I don't mind at all. It's quite all right."

"I wasn't thinking of you," he said with a certain candor. "Can you run this boat? I can't swim."

I reassured him, but not entirely, for he crawled down into the runabout as if he might be going on his last journey. He sat very close to me, but took courage as I cast off and started up the engine. I knew the channel and the markers as well as Tom and Boyd, but we were halfway to Piney Point and the lights ahead were beginning to grow clearer and nearer before Egbert began to relax his caution and his grip on my knee— which was sheer caution, nothing amorous, though slightly paralyzing to my knee. "That girl," he said from the depths of his beard.

"What? What girl?"

"At the table. The Renoir girl."

"The what—"

"The Renoir girl, all pink and white." I thought he smacked his lips behind the beard. "Luscious."

"Oh, you mean Alice. I'm sorry. I'm afraid nobody thought to introduce you."

"Hah," he said jauntily, "we didn't need an introduction. We just took one look at each other—that is, I should say—" He seemed to catch himself up short, but after a moment added, "What's her full name?"

"Alice Warren."

"Alice—wait a minute! Isn't that the name of the girl Tom Esseven's going to marry?"

There really seemed to be no reply to that, so I put on more speed and he clutched my knee again and we arrived at the Piney Point wharf in a swirl of spray.

And then the train was late. Egbert said that he really didn't know what he was going to do with himself until the train came, and since the rules for the care and feeding of authors seemed to be in force, all I could do was suggest the café from whence we could see the approach of the train. There we sat

131

while he drank coffee and told me his views of life and again proved that he had a heart of gold, for presently he said, "Leaf Trace and I have never got on very well. But he's good! If Esseven's only stick with him he'll go right up to the top again. Mark my words."

At last the train came, and I waved goodbye to him as he stood on the steps.

When I started the runabout again, the engine gave several sulky growls but finally turned over. The night was very dark and cloudy. The light from Crab Island turned and turned, sweeping through the darkness.

It wasn't much use hoping that Tom had talked Boyd into changing his mind. But the Sahib and John and Tom were not really beaten yet, though the time and delays the Sahib suggested could not go on forever.

The lights on the island were growing clearer—in fact, I could see the boathouse light—when the engine of the runabout gave a feeble kind of grunt and stopped. Immediately the runabout began to heave up and down in an unnerving way on the black water.

I did everything that we had learned to do to start the engine again, but beyond a weak and harried wheeze or two, it didn't budge. I was too far from the island for anybody to hear me call for help, but I tried it just the same, and my own voice sounded so weird and lost across the black water that presently I gave up. It was exasperating to see the light of the boathouse and the low lights outlining the steps and to know that nobody could hear me. There was a foghorn, but even when I found the forgotten button, it no longer worked. Indeed, I pulled or punched everything I could find until suddenly it struck me that the lights on the island were ominously further away and that the boat was rolling rather uncomfortably. At that moment my flashlight came against me with a hard nudge, reminding me of its presence, and I snatched it up.

The Sahib had been stern about safety measures when we were children. There were definite rules; there were life preservers in the boats; we were taught the simple distress signal.

132

I tried to signal the island with my flashlight, three dots and three dashes. I went on for some time, pushing the little knob on the flashlight back and forth, but when I saw that the battery was getting weak I stopped. Now I began to feel really concerned. The light from Crab Island was nearer but not near enough or clear enough to pick me up, even if the keeper had happened to be looking for a derelict motorboat.

I don't know when I became vaguely aware of a kind of shadow between me and Scatawan Island. It vanished, then returned, then vanished again. At first it was only a drifting smear of blackness, too big to be a buoy. It came nearer and then veered off a little; yet it was still only a mass of blackness, and I couldn't even be sure that it moved. There was an odd effect of the unnatural about it.

But it did approach again, and all at once there was something familiar about its shape. The light from Crab Island swept across the sky and the water and barely touched the black mass beyond me. It was the Ark. Somehow she had come adrift and taken her erratic course out of the boathouse and entirely away from the island, out into the channel. There was a fairly strong current tugging at the runabout. I hoped that I was not going to be carried out to sea before somebody became aware of my prolonged absence and set out to find me. I also hoped that the Ark would stay away from me, but she didn't. She came still closer.

Now the lights on the island were perceptibly further away. I looked back over my shoulder; Piney Point was further to the west than it ought to have been. Still the Ark followed me. It was a perfectly silent but determined pursuit and there was nothing I could do about it. She touched the runabout. It was the lightest touch, barely a quiver, but I knew she had touched. I also knew that the Ark was a heavily built old boat.

When the Crab Island light came sweeping around again, there was no more than three feet of water between the runabout and the Ark. I didn't like this at all; in fact, I was suddenly aware of very grave danger as the Ark crept up again and gave a good hard bump, which sent the runabout over to one side. We shipped a surprising amount of water, and then in reverse motion, when we tipped back, we struck the Ark again.

The Ark was not going to give up and drift away, and this could not go on indefinitely. She gave the runabout another really hard bump, and more water washed in and swished around my feet. The runabout could not take much more of this battering, and the Ark could probably stand up forever; I climbed aboard the Ark.

It was not really hard, but it was not exactly easy, for the Ark rode higher than the runabout. But as children we had swarmed over the boats, and my muscles remembered. I also remembered to take off my shoes and thrust the flashlight into my belt. I stood on the seat, waited, hoped I had calculated the right instant and scrambled aboard, thrusting the runabout away from me in the process. There was a sickening second or two before I managed to heave myself over the rail, but then I was there, flat on the deck when the Ark gave the runabout another bump. This time I heard a dull but ominous crunch, as if something had been smashed, and in fact we then lost the runabout.

I got to my feet. I was a little better off than in the runabout, but not much; if Wally couldn't start her engine, neither could I. Then it struck me that there was an oddly sluggish movement to the Ark. In the same instant I knew why it had not been harder for me to clamber from the runabout to the Ark; she was riding very low in the water, too low. She gave a lazy kind of dip. The current was fairly strong in the channel, but there were rocks and shoals nearer the islands. The lights from Scatawan looked quite dim and distant and I didn't know what to do.

Somebody was on the Ark with me. I don't know how I knew that; perhaps I didn't really know it, and yet I jerked around toward the cabin and tugged the flashlight out of my belt and pushed its button. The hatch was open. The battery of the flashlight was very weak, but it was strong enough.

A man's hand and arm hung down from the bare seat of a bunk. The hand and arm belonged to Boyd. My flashlight shot

134

over him; his legs were sprawled at an odd angle, his head was at an odder angle still, and he was dead. It was like Mildred. All his handsomeness was gone forever.

I had entered the cabin without knowing it. I felt the Ark give another lazy quaver and felt something cold and wet around my feet. I looked down. Water was creeping up from the galley; it was shining everywhere.

I thought then vaguely that the Ark must have already struck a rock. I knew that she was slowly foundering; it accounted for the fact that she rode so low in the water and for her lack of buoyancy.

I turned my flashlight toward Boyd again for a second, and then stumbled out to the deck, dizzy and sick. There was only a weak beam left in my flashlight, but I waved it and waved it toward the island, and somebody saw it.

I saw the cruiser's light first as it sped out from the north end of the island, rounded the point and started hurtling off toward Piney Point. I waved my flashlight and tried to call, but I knew my voice could not be heard over the thud of the cruiser's engine. Then, quite soon really, I knew that my flashlight had been seen, for the cruiser altered her course and came straight toward the Ark.

When Tom boarded the Ark, so easily, seeming merely to step from one boat to the other, I was holding on to the rail. I motioned with the flashlight; I didn't look when he went into the cabin. The lights in the cabin cruiser seemed dazzlingly bright. John was holding the cruiser as close alongside the Ark as he could, and I called to him to give me a hand. But I couldn't move until Tom came up behind me. I didn't say anything. Between them they got me across and into the cruiser.

I sat on one of the modern chairs with its bright red cushion and heard the cruiser's engine throbbing furiously and felt its motion. I didn't see the Ark fade back into the limbo of the night.

Tom was at the wheel. John leaned over me. "Tom says Boyd—"

"Yes—"

"The same way?"

135

"The same way."

The island lights were bright and near; Tom brought in the cruiser.

John tied up, and Tom lifted me out and set me on the pier. "Phone for the sheriff, John," he said. "He'll have to get out the Coast Guard, too. The cottage phone is nearer. We'll be along in a moment."

chapter 13

Tom held me close. He stroked my hair gently, as if I were a child. "There, there," he said, "there—"

"But it's Boyd—"

"Yes, dear, yes—"

His arms were tight and warm and hard around me like a wall, and I put my face against him as if I could shut out the black sea where the Ark still pursued her wallowing course. Tom loved Boyd.

"I'm so sorry, Tom." I began to babble. "You see, the run-about engine conked out. Then the Ark came drifting along and—she must have gone adrift."

"She was cast adrift," Tom said. "There was a hole smashed in her hull and a sea cock was open. Whoever killed Boyd hoped that the boat would founder somewhere on the rocks and nobody would ever know that Boyd was murdered. It would look like another accident."

"Who—" I began, and stopped. Mildred and now Boyd.

In the light from the cabin cruiser I could see Tom's face, lifted as he stared out to sea. It was almost as if he were saying goodbye to Boyd. I waited a moment and knew that I must not cry.

He said, "Can you walk now?"

I nodded, and we started off across the beach; I could feel the dampish sand creep up through my thin stockings. When we got to the stand of pines Tom put his arm around me. A

137

light came from the cottage, and John was putting down the telephone when we entered.

The lighthouse keeper on Crab Island had already spotted the two drifting boats and alerted the Coast Guard. The sheriff was on his way and would bring the doctor. "Not that the doctor can do any good," John said wearily. "But he's the medical examiner."

"Yes," Tom said.

John sat down as if his legs had given out; he looked cold in his white shirt; his face was white too. "Tom, we've got to think things over. We can't call this an accident."

The sand in my stockings was bothering me; I remember taking them off and shaking the sand out. Tom leaned against the mantel, his head bowed.

"I don't know what we can say," John said.

"The truth," Tom said. "The truth about Mildred too. Nothing else to do."

John kneaded his chin; his fingers were unsteady, but his voice took on its very quiet but definite tone. "I'm not sure you're right. First I'd better find out just how it happened. Sister, how did you get aboard the Ark?"

I told him; it seemed to me then that I was only mouthing words that were quite unreal.

"I see," John said. "I think we've got to get things straight. Tom, when did you last see Boyd?"

"Tonight, of course. I mean, we left the big house. We walked awhile. We wound up at his place. We made some hot coffee." Tom spoke as I had spoken, a bare, mechanical recital of facts.

"Yes, but then what?" John asked.

"Then? Oh, I could see I was getting nowhere with him."

"Quarreling?" John asked sharply.

"No. Well, yes. Yes, I guess anybody else would call it that."

"About selling the business, of course." John looked sober. "Anybody hear you?"

"No. That is, the two Bronsons may have heard something. They were in the living room. We were in the kitchen."

"Then what did you do?"

138

"I gave up the hope of talking to Boyd tonight. I thought perhaps by tomorrow he'd have thought it over and might change his mind. He'd had more to drink tonight than usual. I went out the kitchen door to avoid Bronson and came back here to the cottage. I thought Sister had gone to bed. I tried to be very quiet so as not to wake her. I was still awake when you came and said the runabout was still out and that you thought Sister must have gone alone to Piney Point." He turned to me. "I couldn't believe it. I was so sure that you were here asleep that I ran upstairs and turned on lights—and well, you weren't in bed, so John and I hurried around to Boyd's pier and took his cruiser. Then we saw your flashlight." Tom turned around suddenly, put his arms on the mantel and his black head on his arms and said in a muffled way, "Boyd! And we had quarreled."

John said, "Wait, Tom. You didn't really part in anger, you know. It was only a disagreement."

"Doesn't make it any better," Tom said into his hands.

I went over to him and put my hand on his arm. He reached out and gripped my hand hard. Then all of us heard a faraway but rapid beat of an engine.

John said quickly, "Now then. You've got to have an alibi, Tom. The sheriff will be sure now that Mildred was murdered and we covered up. He'll find out that you and Boyd had a serious difference of opinion and that Boyd was determined to sell the business. You've got to have an alibi for tonight. How about Alice? Will she say she was with you all the time?"

Tom shook his head. I didn't know whether he was opposing the alibi or the idea of asking Alice to give him a false one. I said, "It would be better, Tom." If it came to his being accused of murder or his accepting an alibi from Alice, I'd take the alibi from Alice any time.

John said, "But you can count on Alice, can't you?"

"I won't," Tom said.

I knew that he meant he would accept no false alibi from Alice or anybody. John said, "Well then, this is our story. I got the Sahib into bed and quieted down. Then I went out and—yes, I've got it. I walked around to Boyd's. I really did stroll around to Boyd's and talked for a moment to the Bronsons and Alice. Then I'll say that I met you leaving by the back way and that we went up to the big house and sat there on the porch waiting for Sister. She didn't come back, so we went back to Boyd's and got out his cruiser to go out and find her. That may have some holes in it, but I think it's all right. Unless the Bronsons or Alice know too much."

Tom lifted his head. I could see his face and I didn't think that John's advice was going to be adopted. John went on, "Now, don't say too much. Let the sheriff see that you are shocked and grieved and . . ."

Tom whirled around. "Will you shut up?"

John shook his head. "You've got to be realistic, Tom. Is it going to do anybody any good for you to be accused of murdering Boyd's wife—*and* Boyd—and hauled off to trial? No jury, after hearing what Sister has to tell them, will fail to convict you. Motive, opportunity and almost an eyewitness." He turned to me. "Of course you didn't really see Tom kill Mildred but it'll come to the same thing."

"But Tom didn't kill Mildred!" I shouted at him. "Tom didn't kill Boyd. He'd never have killed Boyd. And besides, John, I'm married to Tom. They can't make me say anything."

"And that's thanks to the Sahib and me," John said. "Now Sister, listen. I told the sheriff over the phone to come to the cottage. He'll be here in a minute or two. If you want to protect Tom, stick to your story. You didn't see Tom with a hammer in his hand. You didn't see Mildred. Tom is too frantic just now to think sense. You've *got* to think it, and act on it for him. Here's the sheriff."

The sheriff came in, his hat low over his too wise, too observant eyes. He came over and shook hands with Tom and said that he was sorry about Boyd. They had found both boats; the Coast Guard was bringing them back to the pier. He had seen Boyd's body, and the doctor was now making his examination and would be along presently.

Tom's head was up; his gray eyes were very dark and direct. "There's one thing, Sheriff. This proves that Boyd didn't kill Mildred. But she was killed. We've all been lying to you. She was murdered."

There was a long pause. John gave a kind of shrug and settled back into the rocking chair. Tom faced the sheriff. The sheriff said at last, "I see. I'd better have the whole story."

He had the story, but as a matter of fact not quite the whole story, though at the time it did not occur to me that anything at all was left out. Tom didn't spare himself. He told of his quarrel with Mildred and the reason for it; he told of finding Mildred at the pier; he told of the hammer; he told the sheriff the reason for our elopement and marriage, which only confirmed what the sheriff already suspected; indeed, I thought that there was nothing that Tom hadn't told the sheriff, even the disappearing and reappearing hammer and the skateboard. The sheriff said nothing. John rocked and listened. I listened, too, and made up my mind.

The sheriff didn't question me for a long, long time. When he turned to me at last and asked me to tell about finding Boyd, that was simple enough and I told it briefly. I knew the real battle was coming, and it came.

"All right now, Sister—" the sheriff said. "About the night Mildred was killed. You saw Tom—"

I locked my hands together and my wedding ring gleamed in the light. "I'm Tom's wife."

There was another long silence.

John stopped rocking. Tom turned to look down at me. The sheriff waited. But I wouldn't let him make me speak. I looked down at my hands and waited, too, and finally John said, "She's not an eyewitness, Sheriff. She didn't see anybody kill Mildred."

"She's got what we used to call hanging evidence," the sheriff said slowly. He looked as if he had aged; his eyes were grave and stern. "Now then, Sister, answer my questions. What did you see?"

I didn't even say again that I was Tom's wife and would not testify ever or anywhere against him. I kept my eyes fixed upon my hands and wouldn't answer. The sheriff said, more kindly, "But don't you see, Tom has already told about finding Mildred. John heard the whole story that night. He and the Sahib suggested your marriage."

I swallowed hard. "But you have to have my direct testimony, Sheriff, isn't that right? What they say I said can't be admitted in court." I glanced at John. "That's only hearsay evidence, isn't it?"

John gave me a surprised and reassuring nod.

"Well then, that's all I have to say, Sheriff. I won't give any evidence that might lead to court testimony, and nobody can make me."

Tom came over and put his hand on my shoulder. "It's all right, now," he said gently. "You may as well tell him. I've told everything—"

"I won't," I said, and saw myself in the witness stand, swearing to what would be construed as Tom's guilt; it was as clear as a picture.

There was another long pause, and the clock ticked away. Somehow I knew that there were men on the island, boats coming and going. I didn't hear anything but an occasional boat; yet I knew there were alien presences all about us, everywhere. I wondered vaguely what Alice and the Bronsons would say—and what the Sahib would say. He had loved Boyd. He couldn't have changed in a moment, that night, when Boyd defied him.

The sheriff rose. Without another word he walked out of the cottage, his footsteps slow and deliberate. He closed the door behind him deliberately too. It was oddly frightening, that quiet and self-possessed departure.

Tom's hand lay gently on my shoulder. John heaved himself out of the rocking chair. "I've got to go to the Sahib. He'll take this hard. Sister, if you stick to your guns we may get Tom out of this yet. No, Tom, you needn't come with me. Stay here with Sister." Then he left too, and Tom sat down in a lounge chair and stared at the rug.

He didn't say anything and neither did I; we were both thinking of Boyd. Tom said at last, "Go to bed. Try to sleep."

So I went upstairs, but I couldn't sleep, and when sleep did seem to hover somewhere near, I kept remembering the Ark and the ravaged, terrible remnants of Boyd's face. After a while I couldn't stand it, and I got up and went to the stairway. I knew that Tom was awake too, for I could hear him turn, and the squeak of the old sofa, so I put on my warm dressing gown and went downstairs and knelt down beside Tom, and he said, "Sister," and put his arms around me. We stayed there for a long time, not talking, only holding each other close, and again I felt as I had during our marriage ceremony—that it was all real and that I was married to Tom and so we didn't need to talk because we knew what was in each other's heart. I must have gone to sleep in the warmth and comfort of his arms.

When I awoke it was full daylight; I was in my own bed with my dressing gown over the foot of the bed. I had a hazy memory of being half-carried up the stairs. The weather, as usual, had crankily reversed itself; the day was overcast and heavy, and there was a cold mist outside. Tom had already gone. When I went downstairs, there was a note propped up against the coffee pot. "Have gone to the Sahib. Rest as long as you can. Tom."

A fog began to press against the windows, and it was so dark in the cottage that I turned on the lights. It was very quiet; yet again I had a strong sense of feverish and alien activity on the island. I heard boats arrive and depart, but the sound of their engines was muffled by the fog and they seemed far away, as if they had nothing to do with me. But nobody came to question me then; nobody came to talk to me for a long time.

I debated about going up to the big house, and decided against it, mainly because I dreaded watching and hearing and knowing exactly what all that activity meant. If the Sahib wanted me he would send for me. So I waited and paced the floor and thought and arrived at nothing that seemed to provide a safe course of action. At intervals I could not help remembering the night before when I had flashed the light through the open hatch of the cabin, and the night when I had come down the steps and had seen Tom and then Mildred. I had no idea of time, I never thought of it; it was as if time stood still. But of course it didn't; it marched inexorably on, and late in the morning Leaf Trace came to the cottage.

This time he looked as if he really needed some of his pills, for there were little red flames in his cheeks. His eyes, however, were as dull and vacant as ever. He wanted to use the telephone. "I'm going to call my lawyer! They have no right to keep me here. It's murder, I tell you. Murder and a murderer, and I'll call my lawyer and he'll make them let me go. I know nothing about Boyd's death or—why, they say Mildred was murdered, too! It was no accident! They've been questioning me! Me!"

I said, "Sit down, Leaf. Take a long breath."

He sat down, but wiped his bulging forehead over and over and stared at me. "I know nothing at all about it. They can't keep me here. I'll not stay—"

"There's the telephone. Call your lawyer if it makes you feel better."

Leaf stared at nothing for a long time, and gradually the pink spots in his cheeks subsided. "I don't want to do anything that the Sahib wouldn't like," he mumbled at last.

"He doesn't care whether or not you phone your lawyer."

"No, well, nobody else seems to feel it necessary. That is, those two—Bronson and his wife. They've got money— money enough to buy out Esseven's, cash money! They'd get a lawyer if they felt it necessary. No—" He looked at me; at least he faced me but his eyes wandered. "No, you're right. I'll just keep cool and not say a word."

"Leaf! If you know anything at all about Boyd's death—"

"But I don't!" He shot up out of his chair. "I was asleep. Sound asleep until the police came to the house, and all at once they were all over the island and questioning everybody and such terrible—such shocking—oh, dear me, no, I don't know anything about it." He shrank down into the raincoat he wore and said piteously, "How could I have an alibi? I was sound asleep."

"Leaf, I don't think they suspect you of killing anybody. Really, I don't. Go back to the house. Take a pill and lie down."

His enormous eyes flickered as if touched by light. "You think I'm hysterical. Only a fool wouldn't be scared! Mildred! Boyd! I tell you, there's something loose on this island, somebody loose—homicidal, that's what. I'm going out to those rocks on the south shore. There's a place where I can see all around. Nobody can get to me there." He lowered his chin into his coat and left. I didn't like the way he looked swiftly in

144

all directions before he darted down the path and turned toward the pines.

John came over sometime later. He, too, wore a raincoat over his shoulders, and his gray mustache and gray hair were beaded with fog. "I wanted to tell you that the Sahib is all right," he said. "Tom would have come, but they're keeping him busy. The Sahib is sitting out there on the porch, watching everything."

It was curiously like the Sahib to fake a heart attack after Mildred was murdered and after he had evolved a plan to make it look like an accident. and now, when the truth was out, and Boyd had tragically died, to show himself perfectly sturdy and capable. "I hope he's wrapped up," I said.

"Oh, sure." John sat down. "Scarf, coat, everything. Mind as sharp as a needle too. First thing he did was get me alone and ask if I knew anything about Boyd's will. It's not good."

"Tell me."

"All Boyd's stock in the company goes to Tom."

"They'll say it was a motive for Tom to murder him."

"They've said it." John rubbed his face with an unsteady hand. "That's one of the reasons they're questioning him so long."

"But Tom didn't, he wouldn't—he loved Boyd!"

"Yes, but this is a police matter."

"Did you draw up Boyd's will?"

"Oh, no. He got a lawyer for that. But he told me about it, asked my advice and for once followed it. He left his house and personal effects and all that to Mildred. Mildred was to get the income from his stock in the company and an allowance; I don't know just what amount allowance he finally settled on. But the stock itself goes to Tom."

"So Tom now is really the owner of the company."

"If you want to put it that way. Of course the Sahib will have a hand in management as long as he lives."

"Then Tom—then the company won't be sold."

"No. At least I shouldn't think so. The sheriff asked Tom if he intended to sell and Tom said he didn't know, that it was too soon to make any kind of decision."

"Tom will never sell."

145

John rocked. "Maybe not. You do trust Tom implicitly, don't you, Sister?"

A tiny alarm bell rang somewhere. "Yes!"

"Stick to it, Sister. They'll say that six million dollars is quite a sum of money, as it is. They'll say that Tom knew that Boyd's will left the stock to him. And he did know it—he said that Boyd had told him. So stick to your refusal to answer anything. I'd better get back to the big house and see what's going on. Oh, that hammer, the one Tom found here in the cottage and put in the safe, was still there. Wrapped in a kitchen towel. The skateboard was still in a drawer in Tom's room. The sheriff has both of them. If they've found fingerprints, nobody told me. There are so many old tools scattered around this place that I don't see how anybody could say what's missing—if anything." He rose and went to the door. "Anybody's fingerprints could be on that hammer."

"They'll find mine on it. And Tom's."

"Well, that's natural. The sheriff's got a whole crew working this morning. State and county police. They say the district attorney is going to come here and question us all. He says he wants to see the island and the Ark and everything. Sister, stick to Tom. Don't be afraid. It's the evidence the police can produce at a trial that's going to count. That's how important you are, Sister. If they can't make you budge, we may get Tom out of this yet." He went out.

He must have met Alice on the path, for I heard her high voice and John's murmur. She came out of the fog like a burst of pink sunshine; I didn't quite believe it when I saw that she wore a pink raincoat, but it really was pink, shocking-pink and very handsome.

"Good morning, Sister," she said very pleasantly. "May I come in?"

She was so pleasant that it should have warned me, but it didn't. I told her to come in and she removed her lovely coat, but rather to my relief disclosed herself in blue slacks and sweater this time. She tossed back her hair and smiled at me, but somehow that morning she was not quite the luscious Renoir girl of whom Egbert had so smackingly approved. She said at once, "I know the whole story about your marriage. It's

146

quite all right. I think it was the only thing to do. I've been talking to Tom and to the Sahib. You've been very good about this. I'm grateful to you. Tom is grateful to you. Now you mustn't worry about a thing; we'll arrange your divorce just as soon as we can. And I'm sure that Tom will feel he'd like to—well, let's be frank about it, recompense you suitably. Money," said Alice, smiling, "is always a nice thing to have."

chapter 14

I didn't order her out of the house. I didn't pick up the nearest lamp and hurl it at her. I didn't even tell her that I knew she had urgent reasons for thinking that money was a very nice thing. I said after a moment, "They may arrest Tom, you know. They may charge him with murder."

Her eyes flickered but she smiled brightly again and sat down with composure. "Oh, I'm sure that Tom will be all right. Why, the sheriff is an old friend. He must know that Tom would never in the world murder Boyd. They were like brothers! Why, it's unthinkable!"

"Not to the police," I said, and then was horrified at the grim truth of my statement.

"Well, I only came to tell you how much I thank you for all you've done. Of course, one does wonder rather who did kill Boyd. And Mildred," she added as if in an afterthought.

I said, "Yes, one does."

Alice tossed back her hair. "I realize now that your testimony would have been bad for Tom. That's why the Sahib insisted on your marriage, and Tom couldn't possibly have refused the Sahib. He owes him too much. Besides, I'm sure Tom is perfectly aware of your infatuation for him. So he was afraid that because he was engaged to me, you would turn against him and tell everything you saw. You know, a woman scorned."

"It wasn't that way at all, and I think you'd better leave."

Alice looked astonished. "But what have I said? Tom has an

148

enormous obligation to the Sahib, that's true. But he is also in love with me. So he must have been afraid of you."

I walked across the room, though my knees were shaking, and opened the door. "Tom is in love with me. I'm his wife. There'll be no divorce, nothing for you to look forward to. Now please leave."

It was the last of the lies, as it happened. It was a very big lie, but it came out with such cold anger that even to my own ears it sounded like the truth. Alice rose. "But you can't treat me like this! I'm engaged to Tom! I'm going to marry him!" She gathered up her raincoat and her composure. "He'll divorce you the minute he's safe from your testimony."

"That will be a long time," I said. "A murder case is never closed until the murderer is convicted."

It gave me a slight satisfaction to see the little lumps in the corners of Alice's jaws and the way her hands tightened into fists. But Tom's diamond glittered at me just the same. She had the last word too. "But Tom's really in love with me." She took up her raincoat, flung it around herself and walked out. I watched the pink disappear into the fog and turn from the path onto the beach before I closed the door to keep the chill and fog out.

But I was cold; something which had buoyed me up seemed to have disappeared with Alice. The Sahib and Tom had told her the truth of our marriage. I told myself that perhaps Tom hadn't said exactly what Alice had reported, but I couldn't be sure of that, and besides, her basic argument was true: Tom had been in love with her. He hadn't married me because he was afraid of me, but he hadn't married me because he was in love with me. He had married me only because he was so deeply indebted to the Sahib.

I got some wood out of the woodbox. I was vaguely aware of something down in the bottom of the box—nothing that caught my attention, some old dusting cloth, I thought dimly, if I really thought anything. I didn't start a fire though, for I decided to go to the big house myself. I had to find out what was going on.

I took my raincoat and went through the pines, with the air moist on my face, and out onto the beach. Everything was

149

gray. One Coast Guard boat and two police boats were tied at the pier. The Ark had been brought back and apparently had been pumped out; at least she had not foundered. Several men were aboard her; one in uniform seemed to be writing busily on a pad of paper, and another one had a steel tape and seemed to be measuring something. I hurried on through the heavy sand. I was almost unaware of the long flight of steps, but I stopped from habit at the landing.

All at once, queerly, I remembered the Sahib's coming down those steps the night Mildred was murdered. He rarely came down the steps because he knew he'd be obliged to climb them again; yet he had arrived at the pier shortly after I had come upon Tom trying to haul Mildred up out of the water. And he had never said why. Instead he had asked me if I suspected him of murder—something like that. It was like the Sahib to evade if he chose to do so; still, it seemed an odd kind of evasion just then.

But I didn't believe that the Sahib had murdered Mildred, and he had brought up Boyd as his son. I trudged up the next flight of steps and the next, and eventually arrived at the porch, where the Sahib sat, looking as if he were on the deck of a steamship. He wore a coat, a scarf and a terrible old cap pulled down so only his eyes and a fringe of white curls showed. His eyes, though, were sunken, and there were lines in his face which I had never seen before. Tom sat on the arm of one of the white wicker chairs near him. He rose when he saw me and came over and put his arm around my shoulders. "You were asleep when I left this morning. I thought you'd better get some rest. Everything all right?"

Everything was all wrong. I said, "Alice came to talk to me."

"Oh," Tom said. His expression didn't change; he said flatly, "Yes. She knows about our marriage now." That was all either of them said. I loved Tom and I loved the Sahib and I had no place whatever in their lives after my only purpose had been served. It struck me that biting the bullet is not the brave gesture it is purported to be.

The Sahib said suddenly, "Come here, Sister." So I went to him and bent down to kiss his swarthy old cheek, and he said,

"There now. Don't cry. Don't say anything about Boyd now. We'll come out of it all right, Tom and I." He held me away from him so he could look directly into my eyes. "You're our main hope, you know, Sister. Stick to your story, come hell or high water."

Tom said flatly again, "But I've told them what really happened. It doesn't matter what Sister says."

"You're a fool," the Sahib said. "It does matter. Your story is one thing. A good defense lawyer can do something with that—I don't know what, but something. An eyewitness is another thing; somebody who actually saw you with Mildred, who actually took that hammer away from you, that's different. That would be the end of you."

I said, "What's been happening?"

Tom said, "The sheriff and one of the policemen are back in the hell room with Bronson. They've set an inquest for tomorrow."

The Sahib said, "Bronson killed Boyd. He killed Mildred. No doubt about it."

Tom gave him a tired look, and I guessed that an argument had been going on. "Why?"

"You keep saying why," the Sahib snapped at Tom. "How do I know why? Just tell me who else would kill Mildred. Who else would kill Boyd? For all we know now, there was something between Mildred and Bronson—"

"Not Mildred," Tom said wearily again.

"She could be attractive when she wanted to be," the Sahib argued. "She snared Boyd. Why not Bronson? It seems perfectly obvious that for some reason he had to kill Mildred. Maybe she was making too many demands, maybe she'd found out something about him that he didn't want anybody to know, maybe it was something he didn't dare let anybody know."

"Blackmail?" Tom said. "Not Mildred."

"Why not? So he killed her. And Boyd knew of it too, and so Bronson got rid of Boyd. That's the answer. I only hope the sheriff has the sense to see it."

Tom said slowly, "The sheriff and the police would have had an easier time if they'd known the truth from the beginning. Now they've got to go back and try to pin down times and places and alibis—if anybody has an alibi." He looked at me. "By now, even the time when Mildred was struck is not certain. I was sure that she died just as I was trying to pull her out of the water, so I felt sure that she'd been struck only a moment or two before that. But now the doctor says nobody could possibly say exactly when she was struck. She might have lived a little while, not long, but it seems there's a time margin."

The Sahib broke in. "So you see, anybody could have killed her." He glanced at me and said rather smugly, "That's one of the reasons the police are working Bronson over now. Yes, just stick to the stand you've taken, Sister. Refuse to admit anything—that's what I did. As soon as the sheriff started to question me I denied the whole thing. Said I didn't go down to the pier. Didn't see you get rid of that hammer. Didn't know anything about your elopement. Didn't know anything about Mildred until the next morning." He nodded at his own perspicacity. "He didn't get anything out of me. You should have followed John's advice, Tom. We could have fixed you an alibi for—for last night." The Sahib closed his eyes a moment as he thought of Boyd. He opened them again and snapped, "You should have denied right up and down as I did."

"Do you think anybody believes you?" Tom asked grimly.

The Sahib blinked. "Maybe not. But when the sheriff told me point-blank that he thought I was lying and that you and John had told him the truth, I defied him. I said, 'Put me on the witness stand, just try it. See how far that will get you.' Don't give in an inch, Sister."

I interrupted. "Why *did* you go down the steps after me?"

The Sahib's fingers tapped along the arm of his chair. "If you must know," he said peevishly, "I knew Tom had gone down to the beach. I saw him and I knew that he'd help me back up the stairs again. Then I saw you go down, Sister. So I thought maybe this is the time to talk straight to them. All right." He closed his eyes. "Call me a meddler or a matchmaker or—but I always intended you two to marry. That seemed the time to open your eyes and—" He sighed. "That

152

happens to be the truth, but if I can do better than that if I'm ever forced to explain it, I will."

I didn't doubt that. But I believed the Sahib, so I didn't look at Tom. I wished the Sahib had tried to open Tom's eyes a little sooner.

The screened door gave a muted kind of bang and John came out. "It's all right, I guess," he said. "At least I did the best I could do. I got my secretary at the office and read the statement you and I fixed up. They'll give it to the newspapers. I got the office barely in time, though. Reporters were already there and the phone going. I've posted Henrietta to answer here and say that nobody will come to the phone. She'll love that," he said glumly. "The sheriff's still talking to Bronson."

"Bronson's their man," the Sahib said firmly.

Tom shoved his hands in his pockets and went to stand at the railing. A flash of pink caught my eye and I turned to look as Alice and Nadine came around the corner of the porch above the path that led to Boyd's house. Alice looked excited and, which was odd, rather smug and pleased. Nadine looked grim. Her red hair was twisted up a little too hard; it lacked its customary easy chic. She put her arm under Alice's elbow like a jailer and they came up the steps.

Nadine said shortly, "Where's the sheriff?" She held tightly to Alice's elbow, so tightly that the pink raincoat swung back and I saw a piece of paper, folded once, in the pocket of Alice's sweater.

It was a very neat piece of paper; as a matter of fact, it looked like a folded check. Money, Alice had said, is a very nice thing to have. Nadine had known that Alice needed money. Immediately I was perfectly sure that it was a check in Alice's sweater pocket and that Nadine had given it to her. So Nadine had paid for something.

The only thing that Nadine would pay for would concern George Bronson.

I wanted to see that check, but short of snatching it from Alice's pocket, there was no way to get it. It is curious how the mere barrier of manners controls one; I really could not bring myself to walk over to her and seize the paper then and there.

And then it was too late, for John told Nadine that the sheriff and Bronson were in the little room back of the living room. "Good," she said and marched Alice and her piece of paper into the house.

All of us watched and waited, and in a very short time the sheriff and Bronson and Nadine and Alice came out onto the porch. Alice still looked smug and pleased, and Bronson was unashamedly wiping his face. He wore a handsome brown coat and deeper brown slacks; all he needed was yellow stripes to complete his likeness to a tiger, though just then it was that of a rather nervous tiger. The sheriff was as grim as Nadine. "All right," he said to Bronson, "Thank you—"

George Bronson didn't actually growl, but something rumbled in his throat, and Nadine without one swerve of her brilliant green eyes toward us, went down the steps with Bronson walking very lightly and stealthily behind her, still mopping his face. The sheriff looked at the Sahib and the Sahib looked at the sheriff, and in their look was all the deep understanding of a long friendship and the knowledge of each other's strength, too. The sheriff said, "Miss Alice here—Miss Warren—has given Bronson an alibi. Bronson and his wife were in the cottage at the time when Boyd must have been murdered. They were there at about the time Mildred was killed. Miss Warren was with them both times."

Alice's cheeks grew a little pinker and she put her hand on the Sahib's arm.

"Of course, nobody seems to know exactly when Mildred was killed," she said, "but if it happened just before Tom found her, then I'm sure that George Bronson and Nadine were in Boyd's house. I was with them for an hour or so. Later I'd have heard anybody leave. Last night I was at Boyd's house, too. Tom and Boyd had stopped quarrel—I mean talking. They'd been on the terrace, and then they came in and Tom made some coffee. I didn't hear Tom leave. John came in after a while, I don't know what time, and saw us too—all three of us." She looked at John; his face wrinkled up but he nodded.

He said, "But that was early. Just after I'd got you off to bed, Sahib. I strolled around to Boyd's place—I told you all this, Sheriff. The two Bronsons and Miss Warren were in the living room. I came back here and waited for Sister to return. I don't know how long I waited before I went down to the cottage and told Tom we'd better go after her."

"You said an hour and a half at least," the sheriff said.

"It must have been all of that. Of course, I guessed that the train was late and that Sister had stayed with our author until she got him on board. You can hear the train whistle when it comes to that grade crossing just before Piney Point. Some nights. Not always. Depends on whether or not it's a still night."

The sheriff looked at John. "Then you'll give the Bronsons and Miss Warren alibis—for a time which was an hour and a half to two hours before you and Tom set out to find Sister. Do you call that an alibi?"

"Well, in a way. I didn't go back to the south side of the island until Tom and I went to get out Boyd's cruiser. I can't say what the Bronsons and Alice were doing during that time. But I didn't see Boyd go from his house to the beach. I didn't see him or anybody go near the boathouse or the Ark. I sat back in the hell room awhile, looking at some figures. I've told you all this, Sheriff."

"Boyd never drank much," Tom said. "But last night he had more than he was used to. I suppose it was Dutch courage to help him tell us that he was going to sell the business. So he was confused even after the coffee. Anybody"—Tom turned away from us, his voice uneven—"anybody could have induced Boyd to do anything last night. Go out to the Ark—anything."

"The point is, who did?" The sheriff turned back to John. "The Bronsons' alibi leaves you and the Sahib and Tom."

"Yes, I know." John got out his pipe and looked at it gravely, turning it over in his hands. "I can't believe that you seriously entertain the notion that the Sahib killed Boyd. I can't believe that you seriously entertain the notion that Tom killed Boyd. So that leaves me."

He turned the smooth bowl of his pipe around again and put it back in his pocket. I think it was at that very instant that it struck me that John had some plan. He patted the bulge the pipe made in his pocket and smiled a little at the sheriff.

155

"You'd like some proof that somebody from outside—somebody who came to the island and left again, somebody that nobody so far knows about—killed Mildred and Boyd."

The sheriff said, "I'd like evidence of any kind. Here's the district attorney."

Tom went quickly to look down toward the pier, then whirled around toward the sheriff. "What's he doing here?"

"He's here because I asked him to come. He's a friend of mine—and you're all friends of mine."

The Sahib said dryly, "That makes it hard for you, Sheriff."

"As a matter of fact it does," the sheriff said. "That's why he's coming here."

"Nice of him," said the Sahib sourly.

..........chapter 15..................

Perhaps we had all been dimly aware of the approaching motorboat; certainly we were aware of the silence when it stopped. Everybody looked down toward the steps except me; I looked at Alice's sweater pocket, where now there was no neat rim of folded blue paper.

Of course I couldn't be sure that it was a check; yet in a way I *was* sure. In any event, the only important thing was that George Bronson had needed an alibi and that Alice had given him one. Clearly, too, whatever story Alice told confirmed Bronson's previous account of what he had been doing during the time when Boyd had been killed.

But Boyd had agreed to sell the business to Bronson. Mildred had also agreed to sell the business; indeed, she had originated the plan. There was still no motive that I could see to suggest that Bronson had killed Mildred or Boyd. It was true that Mildred might have been murdered for one reason and Boyd for another. But there was not much doubt in anyone's mind that the same person had murdered both of them. There was no proof of this; it was only so strong a probability that I didn't think anyone questioned it.

But why had Nadine paid Alice to confirm Bronson's alibi? Merely to save him the inconvenience of being questioned, perhaps suspected?

All this tumbled through my mind at that moment, but actually I was as intent as anybody upon the arrival of the district attorney. In our state he is sometimes called the county attorney, and he always acts as the prosecuting attorney. He was puffing, red-faced and gasping when he reached the porch. He was small but rather pretentious, and he wore a red and green plaid jacket and flannel slacks. His very cold eyes took us all in as the sheriff introduced him. I heard the Sahib and Tom and John speak, but when the sheriff came to me and said, "Mrs. Esseven," those cold little eyes sharpened. He waved a pudgy hand. "I'll take her first," he said and marched into the house just as if it was his right.

The sheriff nodded at me, so I rose. Tom and John both started forward to accompany me, but the sheriff said politely but very firmly, "Alone," and then opened the screen door for me.

The sheriff led the district attorney and me back to the hell room. Here a young policeman sat, a pad of paper on his knee; he was idly batting a pencil on it, but he sprang up when we came in. The district attorney walked around the long table and sat down with an air of authority. He gave me a long, bright look which I guessed was intended to reduce me to jelly; I felt like jelly already, so if that was his intention it was wasted. "Now then, young lady, I understand you've been refusing to answer questions. This is a very serious thing. Tom Esseven himself admits that you saw him with the murdered woman, with a hammer in his hand. It is my belief, based on the evidence which Tom Esseven himself admits, that you are in fact an eyewitness to murder. I want the truth out of you and I want it now."

The jelly in my knees had relaxed me without knowing it into a chair which already held a box of manuscript, and I was vaguely aware of my discomfort. The young policeman looked as if he felt a little sorry for me, but he had a pencil poised to take down my replies just the same. The sheriff stood behind me. I waited a moment to arrange my formula, and then I said, "I am Tom Esseven's wife. I refuse to reply to any questions concerning him. This is my legal right, here or in any court."

I think the sheriff said, quite pleasantly that first time, "I told you she'd say that."

The district attorney, however, was not easily convinced. His face grew redder and as time passed it grew so red that I began to worry about bringing on some kind of seizure.

Of course, it is true that the mere repetition of a set reply to every kind of inquiry is infuriating. I tried to soften my voice; I almost apologized with my manner. The policeman became bored with writing the same thing over and over again; from the briefness of his notations, I suspect that he wrote, in short-hand, merely "Ditto." The sheriff looked out the window.

The district attorney tried many tricks, all of them, I believe, perfectly legitimate; I only repeated my formula. When the district attorney said that it really didn't matter whether I told what I had seen or not because Tom had already admitted it, I didn't say anything at all.

At last the sheriff stopped the questioning—barely in time, I was convinced, to prevent something like apoplexy on the part of the district attorney. "I think we'd better try this another time," the sheriff said.

I was almost as tired of repeating my sentence as the district attorney was of hearing it. I rose, and the box of manuscript on which I'd been hunched fell to the floor and spilled manuscript paper. I made an effort to scoop it up, and the young policeman said, "Let me," and shoveled the papers back, higgledy-piggledy, into the box. I wondered vaguely whose manuscript it was and said to the sheriff, "May I please speak to you alone?"

Hope sprang into the district attorney's eyes but not into the sheriff's, who knew me. He nodded, however, and we went into the long living room, where I told him about Alice and the check.

"I think it was a check, though I'm not sure," I finished. "But Nadine said Alice was short of money, and she did give George Bronson an alibi."

"All right," the sheriff said after a moment, "I'll see about it."

I gestured toward the hell room. "What happens next?"

"There'll be an inquest. Whatever the jury decides, which may be merely the fact of death by violence, my warrant for arrest will probably go to the judge of the criminal court. Then he'll have Tom—if I arrest Tom—taken in custody to appear before the county grand jury. It's up to that jury to decide whether or not there should be a trial, and if there is a trial, to appoint the time. Then you, Sister, will be subpoenaed as a witness. So think about it. Yes, Henrietta?"

Henrietta was hovering in the doorway, nibbling her fingers nervously. She fluttered into the room, gulped several times and said, "There's a skateboard hidden—that is, it's in Tom's room, he put it under some shirts in a drawer and I happened to see it and they were talking about a skateboard and—"

"Who was talking about a skateboard?" the sheriff said crisply.

Henrietta batted her eyes. "Why, I don't know, I just heard somebody . . ."

"You heard me and Tom, I expect," the sheriff said. "All right, what about it?"

"Well, that Mrs. Youngwell in Piney Point, she's got a boy, Charlie, and he lost a skateboard." The sheriff must have made some motion, for Henrietta speeded up and her words came out jumbled up. "And he lost it near the railroad station and he saw somebody pick it up and I thought you ought to know."

"*Who* picked it up?"

"Well, Charlie doesn't know, but—" The telephone began to ring again, and Henrietta fluttered, torn between the two bits of drama. The sheriff said, "All right, Henrietta. Answer the phone."

She sped away. I said, "Is it the same skateboard?"

"We'll see. The district attorney is waiting for Tom."

When we went into the hall Henrietta was at the telephone saying that Mr. Esseven was not available, and Alice and John were assisting the Sahib upstairs, one at each side. They were almost at the top of the steps, but Alice heard us and glanced down. I hoped the sheriff would talk to her before she had time to hide the check. Of course, it could be traced eventually, but that would take time. Tom was on the porch and held out his hand to me, but the sheriff came between us. "The district attorney wants to talk to you, Tom," he said soberly.

They went back inside the house and I went back to the cottage, going slowly down the steps, clinging to the railing and wishing that I had given Henrietta more attention when she had told me she wanted to talk to the sheriff. I went past the boathouse and the boats there; the men had apparently finished with the Ark, for she stood empty, still a little low in the water and sinister-looking, at the end of the pier.

The fog was heavier with approaching night. Apparently we were in for a succession of sea fogs. When I reached the pines I could see a faint glimmer from the lights of the cottage. One of the pines seemed to move, and I actually thought it was Leaf in his long raincoat. But when I reached the spot it was just a tree, and when I called to Leaf, my voice only wavered out into the fog and there was no answer. Besides, Leaf would never stay out so long in the fog and risk a cold. I remembered the odd flash of light in his usually vacant eyes when he had said, "Something is loose on the island—somebody is loose— homicidal . . ." I hurried into the cottage.

But when I sank down on the sofa I felt no reassurance. Nothing seemed quite familiar; even the old red and blue rug and my table and the stairway seemed strange and different.

After a time I came to the conclusion that the sheriff didn't really want to swear out a warrant for Tom's arrest on a murder charge. It did seem probable that the district attorney wanted a hard and fast case, something as conclusive as an eyewitness. And I was that witness. But since Tom had admitted finding Mildred I didn't see that my refusal to testify could accomplish much.

I was tired and cold and suddenly hungry, for I'd had no lunch. I went into the kitchen and found some bread and cheese and swallowed it with such a dry mouth that it nearly choked me. By then the foggy windows were so dark that they only reflected me, in smeary patches. Nobody came, nobody telephoned. I might have been lost forever in a dark and foggy world. It was like the night Tom and I had found Mildred.

For all I knew they had already arrested Tom. I heard footsteps and ran for the door but it was only John. He said quickly, "They didn't arrest Tom. They've gone—at least, everybody but the sheriff and a young fellow from the state police have gone. The Sahib is still denying everything, says he didn't know Mildred was dead till the next morning. The sheriff knows he's lying. There's Tom's own story and mine. They can't call Tom's story a confession exactly, but it's close to being that." He slid out of his raincoat and sank down into the sofa, forgetting his rocking chair. "Your refusal to answer any questions at all is a help. How much, I don't know, but a help. An eyewitness who saw Tom with the hammer—" He sighed. "We can't have that. Sister, I have an idea. I'll tell them I did it."

"You—what?"

"It's all very easy. Remember those two cigarettes you said you saw in the runabout? You said you saw me there too. So I'll say I was there and alone."

"But there were two . . ."

"I tell you, it's easy. I'll say I saw you coming and that I didn't want to talk to anybody, that Mildred had got me into a savage state of mind. I had my pipe lighted and I was sure that you had already seen that, so I lighted a cigarette just to make you think there were two people in the runabout having a private conversation. You wouldn't be likely to go out to the runabout and interrupt. I didn't want you to know that only one person was in the boat and that it was me. It was instinct, camouflage. I held the cigarette and the pipe a little apart. You went to the house. I was waiting for Mildred. She had said that she was going to try to open the boathouse. When she came I met her and said I'd help her and took the hammer and . . . I'll say I saw red, I'll say I didn't know what I was doing—"

"She must have been there half an hour or so. She wouldn't take that long to try to pry out the hasp."

"No . . . well, that's all right. I'll say we talked. I tried to persuade her not to sell the business. I went into all the figures. I explained to her that in the end it would be a loss. But she insulted me then—called me a silly old fool. She . . . well, I saw red and snatched the hammer and . . . Then in an instant I realized what I had done, so I ran away in the fog before Tom saw me. I heard him coming down the steps, and . . . Then later I helped the Sahib plan your marriage and all that. I had to protect Tom. He was important to the business. But I killed Mildred because I couldn't help it. She drove me to it. I'll say I had a reasonable motive. She was determined to sell the business. The business has been my life. She yammered at me, called me a hanger-on and said that Bronson would get rid of the deadwood, meaning me. So I killed her." John said thoughtfully, "Sounds reasonable. I knew I'd be out of a job and I'd never get another one like that. I'll plead temporary—"

"John, I think you're out of your mind!" It sounded too reasonable; it sounded as if it could have happened exactly that way.

He went on, "Then—let me see—then I was afraid you'd tell the sheriff about the cigarettes in the runabout. You said you'd seen them. You even told me that you'd seen *me*. I came to my senses, I'll say, after I realized what I had done, and I was scared. Scared out of my wits. So scared I turned into something like a jungle beast. I threatened you in the hope of keeping you quiet and I . . . then I killed Boyd. He was going to sell the business, but that's not the only reason for killing him. I'll say he guessed that I had killed Mildred and told me so, and I was scared again. Anybody who murders that way, not really knowing that he's going to do it, gets scared afterward, scared of his own shadow. Oh, yes, I think it'll hold up."

I could believe it; indeed, it was so real that I felt rather cold.

John said, "It'll get Tom off. Let me see now . . . all the details. I'll say that I got Boyd to walk with me along the beach and onto the Ark. Nobody at his place saw me or saw us leave by the kitchen door. He'd had more to drink than usual. I'll say I told him there was evidence somewhere in the Ark that I wanted him to see. I got him there. Then I hit him with —oh, some tool, a crowbar or something. Then I knocked a hole in the Ark with the same tool and set her adrift in the hope that she'd hit some rocks and sink, and by the time they got her up and Boyd out they wouldn't be able to tell exactly what had happened to him. Details . . . let me see. Yes, I'll say I got stains on my coat. With Mildred it was different. She fell into the water. But with Boyd . . . Yes, I'll get rid of that red coat I wore last night and I'll say there were stains on it and they'll have to hunt all over the island for it."

I could see Mildred coming in triumph down to the boathouse. I could almost hear her taunting John as she had taunted Tom and me; I could almost see him snatching the hammer out of her hand. A moment of frenzy on John's part was believable. His later fright was believable too.

"But a jury would convict you!"

John looked surprised. "You don't think I'd confess to all this if I didn't see a way out, do you? I'll confess, explain, plead brain storm, anything. They'll believe me for a while. It'll get Tom off. Then, of course—well, I know you, Sister. You'd try to get me off. You'd break down and tell your story."

"That would only damage Tom. You said so."

"Wait a minute. Don't you see that by the time they have my confession—I'll leave some neat details which I haven't explained and my lawyers can build on for a defense, I don't know just what but I'll think of something—the point is, they'll have me and they'll have Tom and no jury will ever be able to decide who really killed Mildred or Boyd and there'll be a hung jury and—"

"You still believe that Tom killed Mildred. And that he killed Boyd—*Boyd!*"

"I didn't say that."

"You might as well have said it. Listen to me: *Tom did not kill Boyd.* He—"

"You don't want to believe that Tom killed Mildred, but you can comprehend it. You can see that it might have happened. What you can't see is Tom killing Boyd. But suppose Boyd threatened him. Suppose Boyd guessed that Tom killed Mildred. Suppose Boyd, with his unusual drinking last night, talked too much and accused Tom. So it was a risk that Tom couldn't take."

"No, Tom didn't! He wouldn't!"

But I was chilled. The room felt damp and cold, and I rose, intending to light the fire.

John said, "I can't say that I fancy confessing to murder. Two murders. No. But who else is there?"

"I think that Alice was paid to give Bronson an alibi."

John sat up. "What?"

"I think I saw a check in her pocket. I was told that she's short of money. I could be wrong, but I don't think Bronson's alibi for the time of Boyd's murder means anything. And the exact time when Mildred was struck isn't clear—the doctor said so. Bronson could have killed her and then hurried back to Boyd's house."

It is a dreadful thing to accuse anybody of murder; Nadine's clear green eyes seemed to reproach me. John said, "But there's no motive there, Sister. Mildred agreed with Bronson; she wanted to sell the business and so did Boyd. Why would Bronson kill either of them?"

"Mildred because . . . Oh, I don't know why! Boyd because—you suggested it, because somehow Boyd guessed that Bronson had killed her and Bronson knew it and—well, there must be some reason."

"Of course, you see that this gives Alice an alibi too. Alice . . . yes. I think she might be capable of murder. That young lady's got a fierce will, but I can't see why she'd kill Mildred. Unless, of course," John said suddenly, "Mildred and she had quarreled and Mildred could tell Tom something or other that would threaten Alice."

"Only that Alice was out of money. That would make Tom feel sorry for Alice, that's all. He wouldn't have broken off his engagement for a reason like that."

"No. No, but we may be able to make something of this. Two alibis which, if you're right, aren't alibis at all."

It seemed strange that it had taken me so long to see it. I said, "Leaf!"

"Huh?"

"Greenleaf Trace! His books! They haven't been selling. He's in a slump. If Bronson bought the business, Leaf would have every reason to believe Bronson would get rid of him too. Leaf is—"

"Leaf is scared of his own shadow."

"So he'd be terrified. He'd lose his head and strike at Mildred, and then if Boyd suspected him—"

John said slowly, "What's the proof of this?"

"He had a motive." It really is a dreadful thing to accuse anybody of murder.

John said, "You're shivering. Run upstairs and get yourself an extra sweater. I'll light the fire."

165

"No, I'll light it."

"Toss me that pack of matches, will you?"

I struck a match and held it to the kindling, then turned to toss him the book of matches. He had his pipe in one hand and was absently taking a package of cigarettes from his pocket with the other. It brought back to me that moment on the beach when I had seen two lights in the runabout. John had said he'd tell the sheriff that he had held both a cigarette and pipe. Anybody sitting in the runabout could have seen me come out of the cottage, could have seen me against the light from the cottage door, could have quickly lit a cigarette and held it exactly as John described it and for the reason John had evolved: to keep me from stopping to talk and to suggest the presence of two people in the boat.

The logs wouldn't catch; there wasn't enough kindling. I bent over the woodbox and opened it. I think that as I did so I was vaguely aware of an utter stillness behind me. I was actually conscious only of the crumpled folds of what I thought was a cleaning cloth that Mrs. Mapping had stuffed into the woodbox. I looked and looked again and clutched the cloth. It was a red coat. I held it up. I cried, "It's Bronson's. He wore this the night Boyd was killed."

But Bronson would never have worn such sloppy tailoring. He'd never have worn—Then I saw brownish stains, dreadful blotches on the sleeves and up and down the front of the coat. In a fraction of a second I knew the truth. Then I knew that John had moved, just a little, very quietly, so I threw the dreadful red coat into his face and ran past him and out the door.

The fog fell upon me, like a jungle beast too. I knew that he would expect me to run to the beach, run up the steps, run to the big house. He could catch me on the steps. So I swerved off the path and into the pines. There was all that marsh grass down at the end of the island. Nobody could ever find me there.

..........chapter 16..........................

I thought I heard the cottage door close, and then I blundered against a pine tree and the wet branches on my face shocked me into a kind of common sense. Up to then I had acted from instinct, nothing else. But common sense told me swiftly that there was no way to get to the big house unless I went back again and crossed the beach. The jungle beast, who had murdered twice, was somewhere in the fog between me and the beach, listening and waiting for me. So I must get into the marsh grass and hide.

Perhaps later I could find a safe way around the other side of the island, along the path to Boyd's house.

He might anticipate that.

Hide in the marsh grass; make a tepee in the tall reeds. I was still running. The pines began to thin out, so I knew that the marsh grass and all the irregular little valleys and ridges of the end of the island, which looked so flat and was not, were before me. I could see only fog, but to my cold horror the light on Crab Island was sweeping around toward me and I would be silhouetted against it. I fell to my hands and knees. The great ray of light swept closer; the mist obscured it but not enough. In its glow a shrub of some kind came into view near me, and I crawled over to it and huddled down, trying to make myself a part of its shadow.

It was very small; I flattened down. The light came closer; even in the fog it seemed too clear, a deadly enemy intent upon seeking me out. I put my face down into my hands and waited. Something was threshing somewhere behind me.

167

The sweep of light was passing on, shining mistily upon the distant marsh grass. I listened. There wasn't a sound.

The little clump of thorny shrub was too little. I crawled toward the marsh grass, which now stood black and tall between me and the retreating light. Then I looked back.

He had a flashlight; I could see it darting across the grass. I wondered how he intended to kill me. He had killed Mildred; he had killed Boyd; he had found a weapon for two murders. The flashlight moved jerkily across the grass, lighting up the thick growth, so it looked eerily black and white.

"Sister," John called, "Sister!"

I knew that I must crawl as far as I could into the grass before the Crab Island light came around again. The flashlight gave a jerk back toward the pines, and I scrabbled over some little rocks and pebbles and had almost reached the marsh grass when the flashlight jerked back again and actually went across and above me. He didn't see me.

The marsh grass was inches away. I dragged myself closer and the reeds rustled and I thought: But John can't hear that; he can't hear that. I had crawled down into one of the many little inlets. The tide was coming in; I could feel the wet and sticky mud and the slow trickle of sea water. There was the salty, ugly smell of all sea marsh mud. The tide here always came in full and strong.

The Crab Island light came across again. I saw it barely in time and crouched down flat again.

The light came nearer and nearer, and John shouted, "I see you, I see you."

It almost trapped me. My hands seemed to move without my will; I had almost thrust myself up, intent upon running, screaming, anything, before fear stopped me. I didn't move. My heart thudded in my throat as the great ray of light swept slowly, deliberately through the foggy sky and then went on. John called loudly, "All right, Sister. I'm going back to the house. I'm going to give myself up. Don't be afraid."

But he didn't leave. I'd have heard the rattle and rustle of the reeds, and there was no sound at all.

So that was a trick too.

I didn't move. My hands seemed sunk in mud. If he found

me, it wouldn't be much of a chore to get rid of me forever. It wouldn't be difficult in that marshy, muddy wilderness to hide anybody forever.

John cried again, "I see you!"

And he did see me. Light came down upon me through the thin spires of reeds and showed the mud on my hands and my wedding ring. The reeds above me parted and a light flooded over everything. The light was strong and bright, and I twisted around. John was leaning over me but he was strangely silhouetted against another light behind him. As I turned he swirled around, too, and faced the light.

I saw him throw up his arms, a grotesque kind of shadow between me and the light. I heard him shout, "It's Sister. She's running away. Stop her!"

I tried to get to my knees, I tried to scream. The light vanished. John vanished. The reeds rattled and rustled as if somebody was running wildly through them, but then somebody else came out of the flurry and blackness.

Tom said, "Sister," and scooped me up, mud and all, into his arms. Another flashlight came dancing over to us and Bronson's face loomed up in its light. The two of them got me through the reeds and pines, and another flashlight came jerking toward us. The sheriff was holding it, running. He snapped something at Tom and Tom replied and the sheriff ran on. Bronson and Tom got me up the long flights of steps to the house; I can remember the warmth of Tom's arms. There were more lights everywhere, and then the sheriff was shouting into the telephone.

There were lights and people and questions and I suddenly began to talk and couldn't stop. I told everything John had said to me that night and everything he had done. I went on and on and on and *could* not stop, but Tom sat beside me. I suddenly realized I was sitting on the gilded little French settee. Apparently I hadn't known it either when somebody put a glass in my hand, for suddenly Tom said, "Better not have any more of that brandy."

I was surprised to see the empty glass. The room was spinning slightly, coming into focus and then out again. Faces wavered around and disappeared and came back. Somebody

169

said very kindly, very musically, "It's the shock too, Tom darling. It's all over now, Sister. All over."

A face wavered toward me and I squinted and saw Alice, lovely pink and gold and white, the Renoir girl; she was sitting quite close to me—or to Tom. So it was all over and so was my marriage to Tom. That was clear. Then voices began and people moved and I leaned back against the settee and shut my eyes until the sheriff said, "Sister, Sister, listen. Why did John try to kill you?"

Tom replied, "Because she told him that she had seen him in the runabout."

I began to talk again. "It was raining and John couldn't hear me distinctly. He heard only enough of what I said to get the idea that I knew something about Mildred's murder. He was a little deaf and . . . Then later I had to know if Boyd really was on the island that night, so I lied to John—I told him I'd seen him in the runabout. And he came to the cottage tonight. He wanted his coat . . ." I stopped; I had already told them that.

The voices went off at a distance again. Yet bits of what they said were distinct too. Tom's voice: "John set the Ark adrift. Then he was afraid that Sister might meet it or see it, so he came to find me at the cottage in the hope we'd meet Sister and manage to keep her from seeing the Ark. But it was too late. That was a setback for John. When he came to the cottage to call me I turned on the light and ran upstairs to see if Sister was there. He must have seen the stains on his coat then. He barely had time to shove it down in the woodbox. I remember that he was in his shirt sleeves on the cruiser. I remember thinking that I should have given him a sweater, but then we spotted Sister in the runabout and I forgot about it. He had to get the coat back, and he had no chance until tonight. But then when he found Sister there he got the idea that he'd make sure exactly what Sister knew, and that's why he pretended that he was going to confess. But everything he said was the truth. And Sister accused Leaf, she told you that, so John believed he was safe, until she found the coat."

The sheriff's voice came from somewhere: "All the truth. Everything he said. The details, all of it was the exact truth, even the motive."

Alice's voice: "But you suspected him, Tom darling. When, why?"

Tom's voice again: "I suspected everybody, really. But John had a motive, the same as mine, the business. When Sister said she had told John that she saw him in the runabout, I began to think about that motive. John made an excuse to get Sister alone in the marsh and that bothered me, too, so I followed. But I wasn't sure."

The sheriff's voice: "He was afraid of Sister from the beginning. She had seen what she thought were cigarettes in the runabout. He threatened her with a hammer. We haven't been able to identify it yet, but there's such an accumulation of tools around this old place that nobody could know whether or not a hammer—or two hammers—had been taken. But the skateboard . . . I talked to Mrs. Youngwell on the phone as soon as I could reach her. Charlie Youngwell lost one the day Mildred was found and John supposedly went to New York but actually went to Marshtown to fix up an alibi for Boyd. Young Charlie left the skateboard near the railroad station, and he saw a man pick it up and put it under his coat. He said the man had a gray mustache. I was minutes too late tonight. Tom reached them first."

The Sahib's voice broke in. "Mildred drove him to it. He tried to prevent Tom's being charged with murder, remember."

"Because he knew that Tom would keep the business going—remember that too," the sheriff said bluntly.

Again the voices began to whirl around as if I were in the middle of a spinning circle: "Boyd must have guessed. Boyd rarely drank. That night he did. He was confused. He must have accused him." "Boyd said he was going to sell the business." "So tonight when Tom found that Sister had gone to the cottage and he knew John was gone too, he ran—"

"The coat was burning." That was Tom's voice. "The coat was in the fireplace; he must have thrown it there. I pulled it out and saw why. I knew that Sister would hide in the reeds, so I went down there."

Suddenly the Sahib's voice came in again clearly: "Better if you never find him. He can't swim." Better if you never find him. He wasn't repeating it; only the words kept on going around in my mind.

Then somebody said, again with the effect of an echoing repetition, "Not premeditated, not premeditated—" And the sheriff cut in clearly, "It *was* premeditated. He was waiting for Mildred at the pier. He knew she was coming. He was waiting, hiding. He told it all to Sister. He told her exactly how it happened."

All at once my own voice came out very distinctly: "But then he changed. He told me. He said that when anybody had murdered like that, he changed, he became a jungle beast. He said when anybody murdered like that—" Tom told me to put my head on his shoulder and I did and he put his arm around me.

The voices seemed to recede. I had a dim notion that everybody except Tom had gone, but I was wrong, for Alice said, very close to me, "And now, Sister, you can get your divorce and Tom and I can be married."

Tom had been holding my hand, hard and warm, and now he took his hand away and rose. After a moment I knew that he and Alice were gone. I had a notion that they had gone back to the hell room. So now they were together. My hands were smeary with mud, and my wedding ring had a blotch of dried mud on it too. Something black and shining hovered in the doorway, and I saw Leaf, his face ashy white above his long coat. He tried to say something, made a wild gesture, plucked a bottle of pills from his pocket and simply upended it over his open mouth. Then he disappeared and Nadine came in. "Come on, Sister. I'm running a hot tub for you. You're mud from head to foot. Of course I paid Alice for that alibi she gave George! But George wouldn't kill anybody . . ."

The tiger came into view beside her; the tiger looked sick and cried feebly, "*Me k-kill anybody!*"

"Help me get this girl upstairs," said Nadine.

They did, and Nadine got me into the tub and scrubbed. Then she got a huge bathrobe, so big that it must have belonged to Tom, wrapped me in it, put me in Tom's bed and threw an eiderdown over me. I was so warm and drowsy that I couldn't talk.

172

I was asleep, but I was half awake too, for I knew that some-body was near me, talking. "Alice was a little upset after you talked to her. But there's no heartbreak there, so don't worry."

It was two people, Tom and the Sahib. Tom said, "I'm not worrying about that. Alice was really a very good sport about it all, though."

The faintest chuckle came from the foot of the bed, the Sahib's chuckle. "I gave her a sizable check."

"She wouldn't have asked for that!"

"Well, in my time there were breach-of-promise suits. Per-haps it's different now. Still, she took the check. Oh, yes, she asked me for Egbert Drippley's address and whether he made much money. But she wants to keep the diamond you gave her."

I was too drowsy to take in the meaning of anything until I heard that last. My eyes flew open and I sat up.

"She can't have it till we're divorced!"

Tom was sitting on the edge of the bed. "Oh, don't talk like that, Cornelia! You're my wife."

He hadn't called me Cornelia since he'd had to, while we were being married. I sat up straighter. The Sahib drifted out of the room.

"Well, you *are* my wife," Tom said. "I knew it when we were getting married. I mean, I knew I wouldn't have married you unless I was in love with you. And you're in love with me. Don't try to tell me you're not. You wouldn't have married me if you hadn't been."

"But—"

"Alice? Well, I was wrong, that's all. She doesn't really care, you know. I'm never going to let you have a divorce."

I think I just looked at him and he looked at me and I was very happy. He took my hand and put the wedding ring and my hand against his face.

Again we spend the winters in the house on Seventy-second Street and the summers at the island. Nobody can check mem-ory; it is a part of life. Sometimes I think I see the dark shape of the Ark drifting sluggishly out into the sound, but that's impossible because she was taken away long ago. Sometimes I think I hear Boyd's laugh coming out of the sea fog, but it is only for a moment.

John was found by the Coast Guard. He had drowned, they said, the night he disappeared, running through the reeds. The tide had come in, full and strong.

There are no ghosts. The marshy end of the island looks smooth and green and capable of keeping secret any of its memories.

ABOUT THE AUTHOR

MIGNON EBERHART'S name has become a guarantee of excellence in the mystery and suspense field. Her work has been translated into sixteen different languages, and has been serialized in many magazines and adapted for radio, television and motion pictures.

For many years Mrs. Eberhart traveled extensively abroad and in the United States with her husband, an engineer. Now they live in Westport, Connecticut, where she is a member of the Guiding Faculty of the Famous Writers' School. *Witness at Large* is her forty-third book.